D1373155

JIGGY

by

Jason A. Spencer-Edwards

JASP Publishing Inc.
Queens, New York

Published by JASP Publishing Inc.
133-16 230th Street, Queens, New York 11413
Email address: jasps@msn.com

Edited by: Betty Dobson, Lindsay Young, Joseph Tatner, Jason A. Spencer-Edwards and Kateline Gresseau

International Standard Book Number (ISBN): 0-9713307-0-0

ACKNOWLEDGEMENTS

First and foremost, God. I would also like to thank Kateline Gresseau, Fay, Cyril, and Machael Edwards.

O n the first day of September, the irritating buzzing of my alarm clock awakened me. Half asleep, I reached for my night table and turned the alarm off. It was seven o'clock in the morning. I thought I had set my alarm last night for 6 a.m. I slowly got out of my bed, headed to the basement, and turned on the iron. The procedure was frustrating because the iron took several minutes to warm up. I never understood why my mother loved that iron so much.

I ran back upstairs and began searching through my closet for something to wear to school. I quickly realized I had nothing new to wear. At that moment, nothing seemed worse than showing up to school in my whack, outdated clothes.

I took my clothes to the basement and laid them on the ironing board. Before school, I usually ate light, so I went to the kitchen for some breakfast. I opened the refrigerator and took out the milk carton. As I searched for a bowl to put my cereal in, Tyrone, my younger brother, came into the kitchen.

"What's up, bro? May I have some cereal?"

I opened the cupboard and found the cereal box. When I opened it, I realized there wasn't enough cereal for half a bowl. I said, "Hold on, I'll go to the store and get some for you."

I began putting on my sneakers at the front door. I should have known better; my younger sister Tonya was at the top of the stairs. Tonya usually got up when she saw that Tyrone wasn't in bed. Tyrone and Tonya slept in the same room. They were like fire and smoke. If you saw one, you saw the other. When Tonya spotted me, she said, "Gerald, could you get Munchies? I don't like Sugared Wafers."

I was annoyed at first, but I loved my brother and sister, and there was nothing I wouldn't do for them. I looked in my pocket and realized that I didn't have enough money for anything.

I heard a creaking noise coming from upstairs. I knew it was one of my parents. I listened closely to the footsteps and recognized my father's heavy walk. My father sounded like he was heading to the bathroom. I yelled upstairs, "Dad, can I have some money to buy cereal?"

He yelled back, "What? Gerald, I just bought cereal yesterday."

We were making a lot of noise. Soon, I heard a second creak followed by lighter footsteps. My mother was awakened and standing at the top the stairs. "What's all that noise downstairs?"

My father made his way to the top of the stairs and responded, "These kids seem to inhale cereal. I just bought some yesterday."

My mother responded, "Sweetie, don't forget when you were young how much food you used to eat."

Dad always seemed cheap when it came to spending money. My mother said, "Gerald, go into my purse and get some cereal for everyone."

I searched in her purse and took out a twenty-dollar bill. I went to the backyard and got my bike. I had quite a journey ahead of me. The supermarket was about fifteen blocks away. I looked at my watch and knew time wasn't on my side.

I hopped on Speedy, which was the name I had given to my ten-speed bicycle. Speedy was pink, but I didn't mind because I really loved my bike. Speedy had seen me through some really tough situations. Anytime I needed Speedy, he always had my back.

I started pedaling slowly down the block. I didn't like many things about my old neighborhood, but having a Bodega on almost every corner would have definitely made things easier. I passed the laundromat and waved to Mr. Chin, who was sweeping the sidewalk. Then I passed Mr. Roberts, who owned a flower shop. I saw my friend Max unpacking boxes from his father's van. Max yelled, "Yo, Gerald! You want to play some ball later on when you come from school?"

I hollered back, "Yo! That's cool. I'll check you later!"

I hadn't played ball for a couple of days, so I was looking forward to playing. Twenty minutes later and after some hard pedaling, I was close to the supermarket. When I reached the store, I was completely out of breath.

I chained my bike up in front of the supermarket, next to the entrance where all the candy machines were. If anyone was going to steal my bike, I was going to make it as hard as possible. I wasn't taking any chances with Speedy.

I found the cereal aisle, grabbed the Munchies and Sugared Wafers, and made my way to the cash register. The cashier was checking out customers at what seemed like a snail's pace. I just stood there thinking how late I would be for school. After waiting for what seemed like forever, I paid for the cereal and made my way to Speedy. As I got onto my bike, I mumbled, "Speedy, get me home in ten minutes."

Speedy and I had a very special relationship. When I talked, Speedy always listened. We were moving along very quickly. Every time I pedaled, it felt like I wasn't trying hard at all. Before I realized it, Speedy and I were in my backyard. I hopped off Speedy and laid him down carefully. With the supermarket bag in my hand, I went through the back door. I screamed, "Mommy, could you please give Tyrone and Tonya their cereal?"

My mother replied, "Okay, son."

I ran upstairs and went straight to the bathroom. I showered, brushed my teeth, and washed my hair all at the same time. I had left a trail of clothes on the bathroom floor. I almost slipped coming out of the shower. I began searching for my watch, and I found it buried under my pants. The time was five minutes to eight. With my towel around my waist, I headed downstairs and realized I had left the iron on. I was lucky the whole house hadn't burned down! I quickly ironed my clothes and put them on.

All I needed was my backpack and my sneakers. I got my backpack, went back in the bathroom, threw my clothes in the hamper, and put on my sneakers. As I began tying my laces, I became disgusted as I saw how whack my sneakers looked on my feet. I came out the bathroom and shouted downstairs to my mother, "Mom, I need a new pair of sneakers!"

"What do you mean, Gerald? I just bought those sneakers four months ago."

"I know, Mom, but these are so ugly, and no one is wearing these sneakers anymore."

I knew I was pushing it a little, and she cut the conversation short. "Son, I don't have time to discuss this with you now."

I was really angry, and, to top it off, my father got involved in the conversation. "Gerald, what is your problem? Are you going to school to look good, or are you going to put something in your head? Don't make me get upset this morning!"

I knew it would be a losing battle with my parents, especially my father. I felt brave, so I decided to try anyway. "Dad, everyone in school is going to be looking jiggy today."

My father looked puzzled so I decided to educate him. "Dad, 'jiggy' means fresh, you know? Up-to-date." My father still looked lost. "Dad, the latest fashions," I explained.

He took a deep breath and said, "Well, son, looking 'jiggy' isn't the most important thing in the world."

I knew I was going nowhere fast. Everyone young knew that being jiggy was the key to being popular. My father looked at his watch and said, "You're going to be late for school. We'll talk about this later."

I was tired of hearing that last line. That was the thing I hated most about my parents. If they had handled things as soon as they arose, I would have been the happiest boy in the world.

I ran upstairs and got my keys. Tyrone saw me outside my room and came running up to me. "Gerald, I love you, big brother," he said with a big smile.

I liked to play fight with Tyrone, so I grabbed him in a headlock and responded, "I love you, too."

Here came smoke. Tonya came running down the hallway and jumped into my arms and hugged and kissed me. I put her down, kissed her on the cheek, and made my way downstairs. My mother was still in the kitchen. As I walked up to her, she asked, "Do you have lunch money?"

I had totally forgotten about lunch money. My mother told me that I could keep the change from the cereal. I was surprised she gave it to me without one of her infamous money speeches.

As soon as I turned around, she began talking. "Gerald, money doesn't grow on trees. Don't buy any candy in or out of school. I will not pay for any fillings this year. Do you hear me?"

I nodded in agreement. I hated when the dentist drilled in my mouth. It was very painful, and I didn't want to experience that again. I looked at my watch and saw it was 8:15. That meant I had missed the 8:10 bus. If I wanted to be on time, my father was my only option. I went into the living room, and he was sitting on the couch drinking his coffee. I asked, "Dad, could you give me a ride to school?"

My father looked at his watch and told me to meet him outside. Our car was in the driveway; before I got inside, I realized how old our car was. It was not as flashy as any of our neighbors' cars. The paint was chipping away from the hood, and the color on the top of the car was different from the rest because of all the sun exposure. The front and back bumpers were covered with vacation stickers. We traveled a lot, and everywhere we went, my parents had to get those ugly bumper stickers. Before I sat in the front seat, I saw the stain I was responsible for. To a stranger, the seat looked a little faded, but I knew exactly what it was. It happened when I threw up after eating too many hamburgers.

When I had my seatbelt on, my father got inside the car and turned the radio on. He started singing a song that I wasn't too familiar with. I thought, *that must have been a song way, way, way back in the day.*

I turned to my father and said, "Dad, can you change the station, maybe to some music that's more up-to-date?"

He glanced at me and said, "Gerald, when you get your own car, you can change the station to anything you like. As they say, 'When in Rome do as the Romans do.'" My father was good at those sayings. "Relax, son. This is real music. Don't you hear that melody? Not like that music you listen to. It all sounds the same."

I replied, "Dad, I bet you used to say the same thing to Granddad when he was listening to his music and you wanted to hear something different."

My father paused for a moment and turned it to the station I liked. That's exactly what I wanted, and we were both enjoying the music as we cruised down the block. We slowly made our way to the intersection. The light was red, and a hot red convertible with tinted windows pulled up next to us. The car was so clean it looked like it had come straight out of a showroom. The sun was beaming down on his chromed rims. The driver had a phat system inside his car. I turned to my father. "Dad, can you hear that sound system? That music is the bomb!"

My father gave me a puzzled look, so I broke down the meaning for him. "'Bomb' means 'cool,' you know, something good."

I felt good. I was teaching my father. He surprised me and said, "Okay, son, so that car must be jiggy?"

I started laughing. "Yeah, Dad. That car is real jiggy."

Since we were on the topic of cars, I asked, "When are we getting a new car? We've had this one forever. How about trading this one in and getting something new?"

He scratched his head and said, "Well, son, I prefer to spend my money more constructively. I have a family that needs support, and being up-to-date is not on my agenda right now."

I realized we weren't on the same page at all. Matter of fact, we weren't even in the same book. I sat back quietly for the rest of the ride.

My father pulled up in front of the school, and I got out. As I made my way up the stairs, I glanced back at my father. He drove off and said, "Have fun at school today, son. I hope you meet a lot of new people."

I was about to start my first day of junior high school. I was thirteen, but I felt like a kid in a candy store. I looked very closely at the school and took in my surroundings. I closed my eyes and had a quick flashback about my old school. There were many times I wished I were in another school. Derelicts hung out, sold drugs, fought, and did other unproductive activities. I had always felt like I was in a war zone. I heard cop car sirens all day long as I sat in class. Something was always going down in the playground, and from time to time I heard gunshots. That was a sound I had accepted as normal. The teacher used to tell us to get under our desks if we heard anything that sounded like gunshots. Funny enough, sometimes we were on the floor only to realize that it was a vehicle's muffler backfiring. Most people in my old neighborhood weren't really bad at all. Some knuckleheads were always messing it up for everyone else.

I opened my eyes and continued walking up the stairs. There were no cops patrolling the school, no graffiti on the walls, and no gunshots. I pinched myself to see if this was real.

When I reached the school entrance, I saw a security guard. He looked like he couldn't stop a three-year-old. What a difference! The security guards in my old school appeared as if they chewed nails for breakfast and you were their next meal. He approached me.

"Hello, young man. What homeroom are you in?"

I had no idea what he was talking about. He asked again, "What class do you have now?" I still didn't understand. "Do you have a program card?"

I searched through my backpack and took out an unopened envelope the school had mailed to me a couple of weeks ago. The security guard opened the envelope and took out the card inside, and I saw it had rooms and numbers on it. I looked at the program card and started feeling lost.

The security guard showed me that I had Mrs. Dixon on the fourth floor. He pointed around the corner, and I began walking in that direction. As I walked around the corner, I heard several kids talking about their summer vacations. I had never seen so many different races before. I felt like I was watching a television show. My new school was like a rainbow. There were whites, blacks, Asians, Latinos, and Native Americans. I was accustomed to going to school with some Latinos, but most of the students were black. As I looked around, I heard, "Yo, you're looking jiggy today, player."

I knew they weren't addressing me so I tried figuring out who they were discussing. Someone who had his back turned to me replied, "You know, that's right. Everything I have on is brand new. I have to keep it hot, so everyone can see who's the man!"

When he turned around, I got a good look at what he was wearing. He wore dark blue pants, a dark blue T-shirt, a green shirt, black belt, black sneakers with a green tongue, a black hat with green coloring, and, to top it off, a black backpack. I couldn't believe everything he had on was the same name brand. I looked down at my clothes in comparison and wanted to trade places with him. The whole school stopped and looked at what he was wearing. Everyone in the school knew him, and they gave him the universal nod that meant, "What's up?" without saying a word.

I wanted to get a closer look, so I slowly approached. He even had on the same name brand wristwatch. Another stranger who was apparently jealous shouted "I bet that your underwear doesn't match!" as he passed in the hallway.

Everyone in the hallway started laughing. He responded, "Oh yeah?"

He pulled down his pants and showed his boxers. They did match his outfit and were also the same name brand. The laughter turned into dead silence. He took dressing to a level that I had only seen on television. I was truly amazed, but reality crept in as the bell rang to signal class was starting. I ran upstairs to the fourth floor and found 4-2b at the end of the hallway. When I entered, Mrs. Dixon greeted me. "Hello, young man. Please be seated."

I quickly scanned the room and saw a lot of empty seats in the front of the classroom. I chose a seat in the back of the classroom. I didn't want to draw any attention to myself. When it came to style, I wasn't even a player in the game.

My shoelaces were coming untied so I bent down to tie them. When I came up, Mr. Name Brand entered the classroom. Mrs. Dixon gave him a disapproving look because he had interrupted attendance. Mrs. Dixon began lecturing him on the importance of punctuality. After chewing him out, she told him to have a seat.

As he made his way to the back, all the girls immediately began staring at him from head to toe. The boys in the classroom gave him the universal nod. He sat right in front of me, and I was overwhelmed by his cologne. A boy sitting across from me asked, "What kind of cologne is that?"

He just showed the boy the tag in his shirt and responded, "Like everything else I have on."

At that point I knew he was The Man in school. I wondered if he looked like that every day. The bell rang, and Mrs. Dixon told everyone to have a good day. I didn't understand where she was going, and I had no idea what to do. I waited until the other students left the classroom before I spoke to her.

As I approached her, Mrs. Dixon asked, "Gerald, what's wrong?"

I was embarrassed but I decided to ask anyway. "What am I supposed to do now?"

Mrs. Dixon smiled and told me to take out my program card. "You're in junior high school now, Gerald. I am not going to be with you all day. I am your homeroom and English teacher."

My program card indicated that my next class was on the third floor. I was so embarrassed. But that was the least of my worries. Being in one class would have made things so much easier for me. I really wanted to go unnoticed for the rest of the day. Unfortunately, I had to walk around all day from classroom to classroom with my old clothes.

The bell rang, and Mrs. Dixon told me I'd better hurry up before I was late. I ran downstairs and just got into my seat before the teacher called my name. I peeked at my program card and saw I was in math, which was one of my favorite subjects.

I took a seat in the front of the classroom. I watched as Mr. Jones wrote some examples on the blackboard. His voice sounded like a megaphone.

"Class, take out a piece of paper and a pencil. You have thirty minutes to solve these problems."

As I started computing my answers, I chuckled to myself.

Playing the math game was a Henderson ritual. Mother and I played most Wednesdays. She gave me math questions and if I answered correctly, I got a treat. She allowed me to lick the bowl after she baked her cheesecake. I wanted to get every answer right, so I could be the first at her cheesecake. To me, this was like a priceless treasure.

My mother always challenged me, and I found that fun. But the best part was that I got an opportunity to spend time with her. Family was one of the few things that came easily for me.

Thirty minutes later, Mr. Jones said, "Class, pencils down. That was a surprise quiz, and the last question is extra credit and worth fifteen points."

I smiled as I handed in my paper. That test was really easy for me. My mother had given me much tougher questions. I knew Mr. Jones gave us that test to gauge what we knew and what he needed to review in class.

I looked around the room and saw that Mr. Jiggy was sitting in the back row of the classroom. He appeared frustrated as he slowly walked up to Mr. Jones' desk to hand in his paper. That test took up most of the period and before I knew it, the bell had rung.

I looked at my program card and saw I had social studies, so I hurried to the second floor. I took a seat in the front because social studies was another one of my favorite subjects.

My father had been reading history books to me since I was a little kid. Mr. Malone started writing down the phrase "American Revolution" on the blackboard. "Can anyone tell me who Paul Revere was?" Mr. Malone asked.

I knew the answer. I raised my hand and waved it repeatedly until Mr. Malone recognized me. He finally acknowledged me by telling me I could speak. I answered in a confident manner. "Paul Revere was born in 1735. He died in 1818. He was an American patriot who, in April 1775, carried news to Lexington about the British coming to attack."

Mr. Malone responded, "Good answer, Gerald."

Mr. Malone started writing down my answer on the blackboard. I loved when teachers did that! The other students quickly wrote down what I had said in their notebooks.

Mr. Malone continued his lecture on the Revolutionary War and its key figures. My day was running smoothly, academically speaking. But when I looked around the classroom, all I thought about were my outdated sneakers and clothes.

The bell rang, and I looked at my program card and saw it was lunchtime. I was starving, so I quickly made my way to the cafeteria. When I got inside, I just stood still and stared in amazement. It was five times cleaner than my old school's cafeteria. The tables were newer, and none had any writing on them. It would have been the teacher's lounge in my old school.

After picking up a tray, I got my lunch and paid for my food at the cash register. I started scouting the cafeteria for somewhere to sit. It seemed like everyone had their own cliques, so I sat at an empty table. Kids were laughing and talking around me, and I felt a little out of place. I hadn't spoken to or met anyone yet, and I wondered if anyone in school realized I existed.

After the bell rang, I made my way back to the second floor for science class. I took another front row seat because science was fun to me and at the same time extremely mysterious. My parents invested a lot of money in encyclopedias. I especially enjoyed reading about different kinds of rocks.

The teacher, Mr. Phillips, asked, "Does anyone know what a sedimentary rock is?"

Once again, I raised my hand and waved it in his direction. Mr. Phillips gave me the teacher's nod. I answered, "A sedimentary rock is formed when a mineral settles out of water or out of air or ice."

He looked at me, nodded, and started another question. "Which are the most common sedimentary rocks?"

I answered confidently. "Shale and mudstone."

Mr. Philips responded, "Very good, Gerald."

I felt good watching Mr. Phillips write my answer on the board. I had to hold in a smile as all the students in the classroom copied my answer into their notebooks.

Half an hour later, the bell rang. On the way out, I looked at my program card. I noticed I had gym class, and I became excited. I knew the chances were that the gym would have a basketball hoop, and I loved playing basketball.

When I got inside the gym, my mouth was wide open. I scanned the gym, and the first thing that caught my attention was the bleachers. They sparkled like a diamond ring as I gazed directly at them. They were so clean I could eat off them. The gymnasium floor was also spotless. All you heard were squeaking sneakers as kids ran up and down the gym floor.

At last, I located the basketball hoops. I felt like I had died and gone to basketball heaven. The school had fiberglass backboards and breakaway rims with nets.

My old school had had wooden backboards and ordinary rims. We didn't even have nets on the hoops. We definitely could have used some breakaway rims in my old school. Some of the older boys frequently broke into the gym on the weekends and practiced their dunking. It wasn't cool unless they hung on the rim after they attempted a dunk. You couldn't even make a shot consistently because the rims were always bent.

A whistle blew, and everyone stopped what they were doing. I turned around and saw a lady gym teacher. I couldn't believe I had a lady gym teacher! All of my previous gym teachers were men. She was about six feet tall and was in great shape. She had to work out at least five times a week to have a physique like that.

I wished my male gym teachers had looked like her. Every last one of them had been out of shape and their stomachs had looked like they were six to eight months pregnant. The lady gym teacher said, "Today is the first day of gym class. My name is Mrs. Julian, and we are not going to get dressed today. Let's just go over the rules for this class."

I sat there bored while she explained the rules for the whole period. It seemed like forever, but the bell rang and everyone headed to the door. "Bring your gym clothes tomorrow! We'll have activity!" Ms. Julian shouted as we exited the gymnasium.

I looked at my program card and saw I had Mrs. Dixon for English class.

I tried keeping my eyes open as she went over how to construct an essay. That was easy for me. I had won several essay contests at my old school. I even won first prize for best persuasive essay in the entire school district.

I felt relieved when the bell rang. Homeroom was next, so I

stayed in the same seat. Mrs. Dixon took attendance for the second time, and most kids talked amongst themselves. The bell rang, and I grabbed my backpack and left school.

I began the two-block walk to the bus stop. After I waited for a little while, the bus came. I sat in the front near the bus driver. The scenery was always clearer in the front, and I watched as people got on the bus.

I sat there motionless, replaying my pretty uneventful first day. But the only thing that made it not a total disaster was how phat the gym looked. My stop was approaching, so I rang the bell.

I got off the bus and walked down the block. As I got to Mr. Roberts' flower shop, I saw Max outside sweeping the sidewalk. Max was one of the few people I knew in the neighborhood. I had gone into his father's shop about two months ago to buy flowers for my mother's birthday. Max helped me pick a beautiful arrangement and even gave me a discount. Ever since that day, we'd been close. Max was the older brother I never had.

Max spotted me and said, "Are we playing ball today or what?"

I responded, "Hold up, man. Let me go home and change my clothes."

I ran down another block. When I got inside, I went upstairs to my room. The house was very quiet because no one was home yet. My father always got home later in the evening, and my mother had to pick up Tyrone and Tonya from their first day of school. Tonya was six years old and in the first grade; Tyrone was seven years old and in the second grade.

I quickly got undressed and left my school clothes scattered on the floor. I put on my shorts and a T-shirt and headed downstairs to the dining room.

I scribbled a note telling my parents that I was going to the park with Max and that I'd be home soon. This was another Henderson ritual. In my old neighborhood, things frequently happened, so if I had to go anywhere, I left a note.

I put on my sneakers, locked the door, and made my way up the block. Max was at the end of the block screaming, "Hurry up, Gerald! I am going to take you to this park where the competition is much tougher than you're used to."

I responded, "Please, Max. I'm ready. I'm going to run circles around those clowns."

Max just looked at me and said, "Okay, Gerald. I hope you brought your 'A' game with you."

I hopped into Max's father's delivery van, and we drove off. I became restless just sitting in the van. It was always quiet in the van because Max never drove with the radio on. He told me he liked to concentrate while he was driving. After a twenty-five-minute ride, we arrived at the park. When we walked over to the courts, teams were already playing. Max asked, "Who's got next game?"

Someone on the court hollered, "You do!"

After a short game, Max and I got on the court. We picked three guys who were waiting with us on the sidelines. I loved playing full-court basketball because I had a lot of room to operate. I especially enjoyed playing on Max's team.

Max told me he had played basketball at a Division 1 college before dropping out to help his father's struggling business. Max was six-foot-four and built like a linebacker. He looked like a giant compared to me because I was only five-foot-three. But what I lacked in size I made up with confidence. I felt no one on the court could defend me when I was on my game.

Max usually barked instructions to me as we played because I would lose concentration and make silly mistakes on the court. Max had way more basketball experience than I, so I didn't mind when he told me what to do.

Since we were the challengers, the other team gave us the ball first. Max surprised me when he told me he was going to let me play the point guard position. That was unusual because most of the time someone else had that responsibility.

The point guard was the person who directed the offense, which made it the most important position on the court.

Whoever played that position controlled who got the ball. I took the challenge, even though my confidence began to fade.

The game began, and I dribbled the ball up and down the court, passing the ball to my teammates. On the defensive end, I was very active and came up with several steals. The other team had won six games in a row and appeared shocked.

I was the smallest guy on the court, but I was playing like a giant. Everyone else on the court was over six feet tall, and they thought that I would be intimidated.

I did everything quickly, like I was riding Speedy. When they scored a basket, we also came back and scored. After trading baskets, the score was eleven apiece.

We all knew that whoever scored the next basket would win because game was twelve. Everyone on the court looked focused. I had never played in such an intense game. The pressure was killing me. Even though I tried not to show it, I was really nervous. Max noticed I was nervous. When he passed me the ball, he whispered in my ear, "Weigh your options before you make a decision."

I dribbled up the middle of the court, and one defender came running toward me. I quickly dribbled the ball around my back to elude him. Then another defender approached and reached for the ball, and I quickly put it through my legs to get past him. Then another defender approached, and I crossed the ball over from my right hand to my left hand and left him standing there like he was stuck in quicksand. With all those moves, I came face to face with their center, who appeared to be six-foot-ten. I dribbled toward him at full speed then spun around him. I thought I had lost him for sure. The center recovered quickly and was right back in front of me.

I looked over at Max, who was running down the baseline. We made eye contact, and that was our signal for our secret play. I gave the center a head fake, and he thought that I was about to shoot the ball. He quickly got off his feet to block my shot. I waited until he was on his way down then I threw the ball up in the air toward the basket. Max spun off his defender and jumped up to meet the pass. The pass was perfect, and Max caught the ball in the air and dunked it. All you heard was a loud thump as the ball went crashing through the basket. I put my fist in the air and screamed, "Yes! Yes! Yes!"

Max came running over to me and gave me a high five. That was the first time we had successfully completed that play. We had tried several times before, but something had always gone wrong.

The basketball gods were definitely shining their light on me. People on the sidelines were jumping up and down. Someone shouted, "Yo! Yo! Shorty threw an ill alley-oop!"

Our opponents came over to congratulate me, and I knew I

had earned their respect. I looked over to the sidelines and saw some familiar faces from school. I walked over to the sidelines to get a better look. "Aren't you the new boy in school?" one of the boys asked.

"Yeah," I responded.

He said, "My name is John. That's Bill, and that's Steve."

I did a double take because Steve was the one in school who was Mr. Jiggy. I stared at him. He was jiggy from head to toe. He wore red sneakers, white socks, red shorts, a white T-shirt, a red headband, and white wristbands. His sneakers alone were $175.

Max got my attention and said, "Gerald, we have to go! You are going to be late."

I told Bill, John, and Steve that I would see them tomorrow in school. John and Bill said, "Later, Gerald. See you tomorrow."

Steve's lips didn't move, as if to say I wasn't important at all. He just nodded his head like he was too cool to speak.

As we drove home, Max said, "You definitely brought your 'A' game today."

"Thanks, Max, for giving me the chance to play the point guard position." I quickly changed the subject. "Yo, Max. Did you see those sneakers that kid had on? I saw them in the mall for a buck seventy-five. Tell me those weren't jiggy."

Max replied, "Man, please. When you're balling, you don't

worry about sneakers. You're playing for the love of the game."

"I know, but those are hot," I answered.

"Let me ask you something. Did you see any of those guys playing basketball?"

I thought for a second and responded, "No."

Max shook his head. "Exactly. It isn't always about looking jiggy."

That comment sounded like something my Dad would have said. "Whatever, Max. Those are still jiggy."

He shook his head again. "You'll learn."

Max pulled up in front of my house and gave me another high five. As soon as I walked through the door, Tyrone jumped on me. "Gerald's home! Gerald's home!"

My sister Tonya, who was sitting on the floor playing with her doll, imitated Tyrone and screamed, "Gerald's home! Gerald's home!"

My mother walked into the living room and told me to get ready for dinner. I went upstairs and jumped in the shower because I smelled terrible.

While Gerald was showering, his father came in and was greeted with, "Daddy's home, Daddy's home!" from Tyrone and Tonya.

Gerald's mother greeted her husband with a kiss. "How was your day at work?"

"Sweetie, it was busy. I didn't get a chance to take lunch."

Gerald's father was a construction worker, and his company was working on a new skyscraper downtown. "Honey, how was your day?"

"Busy as usual, patients coming in and out of the hospital."

Gerald's mother was a registered nurse who also worked downtown. If they weren't busy during the day, they got together at lunchtime. Gerald's father sat down on the couch, and Tyrone and Tonya fought to help their father take off his work boots. They started a conversation between them.

"I'll take the left one," Tyrone said.

"I'll take the right one," Tonya said.

"I'll race you. Let's see who finishes first. On your mark, get set, go," Tyrone said.

They appeared to remove the shoes at the same time but couldn't decide for themselves. "Who won Daddy?" Tonya asked.

"It was a tie. You both win."

They smiled at each other and continued playing on the floor. Gerald's mother was in the kitchen putting the finishing touches on the meal. "Tyrone. Tonya. Help me set the table."

They jumped up and went to the kitchen. Tyrone's job was to

put the knives, forks, and tablemats on the table. Tonya's job
was to put the glasses and napkins on. Gerald's responsibility
was the plates and drinks. Gerald's mother called him from the
bottom of the stairs. "Gerald, come down and finish setting the
table."

While I was getting dressed in my room, I heard my mother
calling my name. I opened my door and said, "Mom, I'm
coming!"

I hurried downstairs and greeted my father. I saw that the
table was almost set, so I got the drinks and the plates. We
were all seated and waiting patiently as my mother went back
and forth, carrying dishes to the table.

On the table were macaroni and cheese, chicken, mixed
vegetables, and brown rice. My mouth watered just thinking
about the food. The only thing left was for Grace to be said. It
was Tonya's turn to say Grace. "Thank you, Lord, for the food,
my family, and thank you for my doll. Amen."

Everyone smiled and responded, "Amen."

The dinner table was quiet as everyone focused on the food.
After we finished our meal, Tyrone, Tonya and I did our chores
in reverse. Dad went to the kitchen and washed the dishes. This
gave my mother a much-needed break since she usually cooked
the food.

My mother sat on the couch in the living room, and I sat on the floor next to her. After my Dad washed the dishes, he came into the living room and sat next to my mother. "Honey, the food was good as usual." She smiled, and he gave her a kiss on the cheek.

I added, "Yeah, Mom, the food was good."

My father turned to me and asked, "How was your day, son?"

I didn't want to get into it with him, so I responded, "It was okay."

"'Okay'? The first day of a new school, and all you have to say is, 'Okay'? So how many people did you meet today?"

I didn't want to seem pitiful, so I replied, "Not that many."

"How come?"

I was tired of dodging the truth, so I said, "No one seemed to pay any attention to me, Dad."

He looked at me smiled and said, "Well, that's okay. Tomorrow will be different."

My mother jumped in. "How were your classes?"

I became excited because that was one of the few highlights of the day. "Great, mother! Classes were a breeze."

"Oh, really?"

"All those hours you guys spent reading to me and quizzing me definitely has paid off. I answered so many questions today."

My mother said, "I am happy, son. I want you to be prepared for the real world. It's no joke out there. Without preparation and planning, nothing can be accomplished."

I nodded in agreement.

Tyrone and Tonya ran into the living room, giggling and laughing. My mother looked at her watch and told them that it was time they went to bed. She walked behind them as they headed upstairs. They turned back and said good night.

My father became curious and asked, "Do you like your new school?"

I said, "Well, Dad, it's okay, but everyone looks so jiggy. I kind of feel out of place."

By the look he gave me, I knew I shouldn't have mentioned that word again. He scratched his head. "Son, I could tell you why this isn't important, but right now you are not concentrating on what is important. Here's what I'll do. I'll give you time to adjust to your new school and surroundings. If you think being jiggy is still important to you, we'll come up with a solution."

That sounded reasonable to me. "Okay, Dad."

I went upstairs and walked by the bathroom. Tyrone and Tonya were brushing their teeth as my mother watched over them. I went to my room and lay in bed for about twenty minutes before I fell asleep.

My alarm clock woke me up, and that was the beginning of the second day of school. I almost smashed the clock as I tried turning it off. I wasn't looking forward to going to school. Slowly, I headed toward the bathroom and started my morning routine. The shower woke me up a little, but I still wanted to stay home. I ran downstairs and turned on the iron. I came back upstairs and picked the closest outfit in my closet. I went back downstairs and ironed my clothes. I put my clothes on while I was in the basement. As I looked at my outfit – blue pants, a green shirt, a brown belt, and gray sneakers – I felt disgusted. I ran back upstairs to my room and found my hat. The red hat wasn't a matching addition to my already colorful outfit. I was a fashion disaster. If the fashion police had ever seen that outfit, they would have locked me up and thrown away the key.

When I got downstairs, I grabbed my backpack. Suddenly, I heard a faint creaking sound. It was amazing how I knew certain sounds in my house. It had to have been either Tyrone or Tonya going to the bathroom. I was ahead of schedule, so I left and slowly headed down the block. As I reached the end of the block, I saw Max unloading boxes in front of his father's flower shop. Max said, "What's up, All-Star? Can I have your autograph?'"

I took out a piece of paper and wrote my name on it. I told him he should keep it just in case it's worth something one day. Max looked at me and couldn't stop laughing. I continued walking toward the intersection and saw the bus coming around the corner. I ran across the street and just caught the bus before the bus driver closed the doors. The bus was packed with people heading to school and work. This was the first time I had ridden the bus to school.

I stared out the window as the bus drove along. Everyone on the street seemed to be in a good mood. That's what made suburban life so laid back. No one seemed to have a care in the world.

In my old neighborhood, people always looked upset. If you saw someone smiling, you wondered whether they were on drugs or something. Besides, smiling was seen as a sign of weakness. That happy-go-lucky attitude usually got you robbed. I used to practice my mean face in the mirror all the time and it had gotten me out of a lot of situations. I was lucky I wasn't tested. There were many times I had been scared to death. I could put my mean face away because my new neighborhood was much safer and friendlier.

My stop approached, and I rang the bell. As I got closer to the school, I heard kids talking and laughing. Bill, John, and Steve were standing in front of the school. I moved closer toward them.

Bill and John said, "What's up, Gerald?"

"What's up, guys?"

Steve's mouth remained closed. He just looked in my direction and nodded his head. I gave his outfit a thorough examination. His colors were gray and black: black pants, gray shirt, black belt, black and gray sneakers, black watch, gray book bag, and gray hat with black lettering.

The bell rang, and everyone went to homeroom. I made my way to the back of the classroom. Steve sat in front of me, as he had done yesterday, while Mrs. Dixon called attendance.

When I looked at the front of the classroom, I saw two students passing around what appeared to be some kind of flyer. I wondered what was on the flyer.

I wanted to know badly, but since I didn't know them I dared not ask. It was embarrassing enough that I had on whack clothes and sneakers. I certainly wasn't going to give anyone the opportunity to disrespect me as well.

As the day carried on, I went to math, social studies and science. In science class, Mr. Malone announced, "Class, I want you to work on a science project. It is due three months from now. Everyone should have a partner and discuss what you'll be working on. This science project will count for fifty percent of your final grade. So everyone has to pull their own weight. Remember, class, this is a team effort."

Someone from the back of the class asked, "Can we pick anyone we want?"

Mr. Malone replied, "Well, class, it has been my experience that we pick people we like or someone who will do most, if not all, of the work. To avoid this, I will select partners, and that person is the one you'll be working with."

The class showed its disapproval by talking. Mr. Malone switched the lights off then back on and said, "Quiet! Class, quiet! My decision is final."

Mr. Malone went row by row and gave everyone a partner. I could not figure out his formula. Everyone was mixed up. Boys were teamed with girls and even different races were paired up.

Mr. Malone finally called my name. "Gerald, you are to pair up with Steve."

Mr. Malone told the class to introduce themselves to their partner. I went over to Steve and said, "Hello, my name is Gerald."

Steve didn't respond. He just nodded his head.

"When do you want to start this project?" I asked.

Steve looked at me and finally spoke. "What's your name again?"

I didn't see a hearing aid, so I knew he wasn't hard of

hearing. I repeated myself. "Gerald."

He answered sarcastically, "Okay, Gerald. After school, you can come to my house, and we'll get started."

As I walked back to my seat, the bell rang.

On Tuesdays, my schedule was slightly different; instead of having lunch before science class, I had lunch after science class. I entered the lunchroom, and the scene hadn't changed. Everyone still sat with their cliques. I felt like an outcast. I got my lunch and walked over to an empty table. As soon as I sat down, someone shouted, "Yo, Gerald! Over here."

I looked in every direction, but I couldn't quite tell where the voice was coming from. Again I heard, "Yo, Gerald! Over here."

I looked around again and realized that the voice was coming from a table where Bill, John, and Steve were sitting. They were the only ones there. I slowly approached the table. When I got in front of the table, Bill said, "Gerald, bring your lunch and come sit with us."

I went back to my table, grabbed my lunch, and headed back to where they were sitting. As I walked, I noticed a lot of kids staring at me. I sat down, and Bill and John gave me high fives. Steve just nodded, as usual.

Bill asked, "Where did you learn to play ball like that? You're really good!"

"I learned from my Granddad and my friend Max."

Bill said, "Man, I wish Max could teach me. You really put on a show."

John interrupted, "Yeah, man, you definitely got game."

Steve just nodded. Steve didn't seem to like the attention I was getting and quickly switched the conversation. "Fellows, did you see those new sneakers on the billboard?"

Bill said, "Yeah, those are jiggy."

Steve replied, "I'm getting them today."

John said, "Aren't those about $160?"

"And? Trust me, I'll be wearing them tomorrow."

I had no idea what they were talking about. I hadn't seen any sneaker billboard on the way to school. As I looked around, four girls approached the table.

As if they had practiced this several times the night before, they said, "Hello, Steve!"

"Hi, ladies."

After they left, Bill tapped John and said, "Those girls sure are cute. What do you think, Gerald?"

I said, "I agree with you. They are definitely pretty."

Steve interrupted. "It's quite simple. I'm the man in this school. Who doesn't know that? I'm the top dog in this place."

Bill agreed and smacked Steve's hand, and John joined in. Another student came to the table and asked Steve, "That shirt is fire. What kind of shirt is that?"

"Take a look at the tag."

He looked and said, "Can I ask how much it cost?"

"If you have to ask, that means you can't afford it."

The boy was embarrassed and walked away with his head down.

I looked carefully at Bill and John's clothing. They were also wearing new clothes, but you could tell theirs weren't as expensive as Steve's. When it came to clothing, Steve definitely dressed the best. Bill and John were like his protégées, and they were happy to be around him. He generated a lot of attention, and, for the first time, people realized that I also existed. It seemed liked the whole cafeteria was looking at me. I talked with the guys until the bell rang.

I made my way to the locker room and got changed for gym class. Everyone came out wearing the same thing: blue shorts and a white T-shirt. For the first time, I felt I wasn't any different from anyone else except for my sneakers, which weren't part of the dress code for class.

As we lined up, I stared at the fiberglass backboards. I just knew that we would be playing basketball. Two janitors rolled out a long pole with a net. I was extremely disappointed because I didn't like playing volleyball. But when I stared at the net again, I realized that the net was smaller than a volleyball net. The janitors left, but they returned in five minutes. They rolled out more poles with nets. By time they were finished, there were eleven poles and nets set up on the gymnasium floor. I was more confused than before.

Mrs. Julian announced, "Class, today we are going to be playing badminton. I will explain the rules later, but first let's learn to play. For those who are new at this, pay close attention. Could I please get a volunteer?"

A girl from the back of the gym came sprinting up to the teacher. Mrs. Julian handed her a racket that looked like a small tennis racket. Mrs. Julian went into her pocket and pulled out a funny looking object. It had rubber on one end and a plastic white mesh material on the other end. It actually looked like a miniature Indian teepee with a rubber stopper on the other end. "The object of the game is to hit the shuttlecock over the net without it hitting the ground," Mrs. Julian explained.

Shuttlecock was a new word for me. I realized she must have been talking about the Indian teepee. I looked at the shuttlecock and wondered, *how am I going to do that?* Mrs. Julian and the volunteer demonstrated to the class how to hit the shuttlecock over the net. I was amazed as they rallied back and forth. The girl was really good, and she had Mrs. Julian chasing the shuttlecock all over the place.

When the shuttlecock finally touched the ground, Mrs. Julian asked, "Does everyone get the picture?" She paused. "I am going to separate you into teams. I want one team on one side of the net and the other team on the other side."

I was getting nervous because I didn't quite get the motion of the racket. Badminton was foreign to me. Mrs. Julian made sure that each person's partner was the opposite sex. My partner was the girl who demonstrated the game with Mrs. Julian. I picked up a racket, walked over to the net, and introduced myself. "Hello. My name is Gerald."

"Pleased to meet you, Gerald. I am Suzanne."

Our opponents were Bill and a girl named Denise. Suzanne said to Bill, "We'll serve first."

She looked at me and said, "Gerald, serve."

I didn't want to look stupid, so I said, "You can serve first."

"Come on, Gerald. It's not that bad," she said encouragingly.

I didn't want to, but I said, "Okay, I'll try."

I took the racket in my hand and tried to serve the shuttlecock with the mesh part first and it went crashing to the gym floor.

Bill chuckled. "Ha! Ha! Ha! Yo, Gerald, get it over the net."

Suzanne interrupted. "Gerald, take the racket with your right hand. Place the mesh part of the shuttlecock facing up and the rubber end facing down in front of the racket. After that, give an underhand scoop with the racket."

I followed her instructions to a tee, and the shuttlecock went flying across the net, straight toward Bill. He swung his racket and missed.

Suzanne chuckled and said, "That's one point for us."

My confidence grew as we continued playing. Every step of the way, Suzanne gave me more and more useful tips. I was getting the hang of it, and I confidently ran down the shuttlecock time after time. Bill and Denise were no match for us, and we won each game easily.

Bill seemed a little frustrated and said, "Yo, Gerald, are you sure you haven't played this game before?"

"Nope. It must be beginner's luck."

The bell rang, and Mrs. Julian said, "Everyone, put your rackets away. Class, see you tomorrow."

I caught up to Suzanne on her way to the girls' locker room. "Thank you for teaching me how to play."

"You're welcome. See you tomorrow."

When I got into the boys' locker room, I got showered and dressed. Afterwards, I grabbed my stuff and headed toward English class. Along the way, I saw Suzanne standing with her friends in the hallway. She smiled and said, "Hi, Gerald!"

"Hi, Suzanne," I responded as I smiled and continued walking.

When I turned around, I saw Suzanne whispering into one of her friends' ears. They all turned toward me to get a better

Jason A. Spencer-Edwards   45

look. I knew they had to be saying something good because they were all smiling at me.

The bell rang, and I made my way to my seat. English class went by quickly, and I wasn't paying much attention to the lesson because I couldn't stop thinking about Suzanne. When English class was finished, I remained seated for homeroom.

Before Mrs. Dixon came into the classroom, I saw some students looking at that flyer again and talking about it. I couldn't quite make out what they were saying because they were whispering. Mrs. Dixon came in, and everyone quieted down when she began taking attendance. Shortly after she finished taking attendance, the bell rang. I grabbed my backpack and walked through the hallway. Before I left school, I heard a voice.

"Yo, Gerald, wait up!"

When I turned around again, I saw Steve. He was standing with John and Bill.

I said, "What's up, guys?"

"Nothing. What are you doing now?" Steve asked.

"Going home."

"Are you still coming to my house for the science project?"

I was surprised. "Today?"

"Yeah, man!"

I went to the payphone and called my mother's job. I called

her instead of my father because she was much easier to locate. When I finally got her, I said, "Mom, can I go to a classmate's house to work on a science project?"

My mother paused and said, "Okay, dear. And make sure you keep in contact with me, so I know what's going on."

"Okay, Mom."

In a loving voice, she said, "Be careful. I love you."

"I love you, too, Mom."

Steve, John, Bill, and I walked to the bus stop. When the bus arrived, I sat next to John. Steve and Bill sat together. All four of us were looking out the window.

As we passed a huge billboard on Fern Street, Steve said, "Yo, Bill, tell me those sneakers ain't jiggy."

"Yup. Those are most definitely jiggy."

Steve got up and rang the bell.

John jumped up and asked, "Yo, Steve, where are you going?"

Steve made his way to the back entrance and replied, "I am getting those sneakers right now." He looked at me and said, "Are you coming to the store with us? We'll be in and out in fifteen minutes."

I followed them because I wanted to be around the guys badly. We got off and started walking, but I wasn't sure where we were going. A couple of blocks later we entered a store.

John, Bill, and Steve started speaking to a man standing at the cash register. "What's up, Mr. Smith?" Steve asked.

"You tell me, Steve. It has been two weeks. Where have you been?"

Their conversation continued, and Steve said, "Mr. Smith, I've been busy. Do you have those new sneakers I saw on the billboard on Fern Street?"

"Sure do, and just in your size."

Mr. Smith went to the back of the store to get them. His store had hats, sweat suits, jackets, T-shirts, boots, shoes, and other apparel. The store wasn't that big, but the merchandise was up-to-date. I wanted to have one of everything. John and Bill were trying on sweat suits.

"Hey, Gerald, how does this look?" Bill asked.

"That is definitely hot."

I went over to the sneaker section. I looked at every sneaker they had displayed. I realized the store didn't sell the ones I had on my feet. But the sneakers John, Bill, and Steve had on were there. Theirs were priced in the nineties and hundreds, and they were all marked as "new arrivals."

When Mr. Smith came back with the sneakers, Steve called us over. "Yo, fellows, come check them out."

We all watched as Steve tried the sneakers on. Bill said, "Man, those are hot, right, John?"

"Those are fire."

Steve put on the right foot first. The left foot was sitting outside the box, and I was studying them carefully. Steve caught me staring and said, "Yo, Gerald, you want to try them on?"

I hesitated then said, "Okay."

As I tried them on, I felt like I was floating on clouds.

Steve asked, "Do you like them?"

I didn't want to take them off and put back on my own sneakers. "Without a doubt."

I slowly took them off and placed them next to the box. Steve called Mr. Smith over and told him to put them back into the box. He then instructed Mr. Smith to put a white T-shirt, dark blue pants, and a white hat in the bag. It was like Mr. Smith was his butler. He knew exactly what size to get. When everything was in the bag, Steve got up and said, "Yo, fellows. Let's go."

We followed Steve and left Mr. Smith's store. I got extremely curious because I hadn't seen Steve hand Mr. Smith any money. I whispered into John's ear, "How did he pay for that?"

"Man, he just puts it on his parents' account."

I wished my parents had given me an account in Mr. Smith's store. As I looked up the block, I saw the bus pulling around the corner. I screamed, "Yo, fellows! The bus is coming."

We started running to catch the bus. Steve, John, and Bill were behind me. I knew that if I wanted to catch the bus, I would have to hurry. I ran in Speedy mode. I caught the bus just before the bus driver closed the doors. When I got up to the bus driver, I said, "Could you please wait a minute? My friends are coming."

The bus driver waited, and Steve, John, and Bill got to the bus a couple of minutes later, completely out of breath. We sat together in the back, and John asked Steve, "Can I see those sneakers again?"

"Sure, man."

I remembered how it had felt when I had them on my feet.

The bus driver was moving, and in no time Bill and John rang the bell as their stop approached. As they got off the bus, they gave Steve and me the universal nod.

I asked, "How much longer to your house?"

Steve said, "Don't worry. We'll be there soon."

It had been a very long day for me; before I knew it, I was sleeping. I awoke when Steve nudged me. "Gerald, wake up, man! My stop is next."

I was startled and jumped up quickly. As we walked down the block, I saw several upscale homes. Steve's neighborhood was much better looking than mine. Most of the houses represented how the rich and the famous lived.

As we walked, I watched a lady instructing her gardener on how to plant the flowers. I realized these people really had money. When I looked in some of Steve's neighbors' driveways, I saw some real hot cars. A lot of them were unfamiliar to me, but I knew they were expensive. Every house was sitting on acres of land, and the backyards and front lawns were huge. Steve's neighborhood represented jiggy to the fullest.

We finally approached Steve's house. It was beautiful! The grass was well manicured. The flowers in the front of his house were so colorful. I hadn't seen that many colors in front of anyone's house before.

Steve went into his pocket and took out his keys, and we went through the front door. The inside of Steve's house looked like a palace fit for a king and a queen. The house was spotless, and everything looked unused. I wondered if anyone really lived there. "How long have you been living here?"

"Well, as long as I can remember. Let's see, I am thirteen, so thirteen years."

We took off our sneakers and placed them near the front door. I heard a weird noise from his kitchen. "What's that noise? Is your mother cooking?"

"No, that's the maid."

I was surprised. "You have a maid?"

"Yeah, she cooks and cleans our house three times a week."

"Where are your parents?"

"Well, as usual, they're either at work, some convention, or a training session. My mother is a computer programmer for a big company downtown, and she travels from state to state. She's out of town for months at a time. She's always creating new programs for her company's clients."

I became curious. "What about your father?"

"He's a salesman for a big pharmaceutical company downtown. He sells drugs and accessories to hospitals from state to state."

Steve had a house I would have loved to live in. I looked at my watch and noticed it was approaching 5:30 p.m. "Steve, may I use your phone?"

"There is one in the kitchen."

I walked into the kitchen, and the maid introduced herself. She began talking in a strong European accent. "My name is Mrs. Miles. What is your name, young man?"

"Gerald."

"Pleased to meet you, Gerald. Can I help you?"

"May I please use the phone?"

"Sure."

I picked up the phone and started dialing. It rang three times before Tyrone answered and started announcing, "It's Gerald.

It's Gerald."

"Okay, okay. Put Mom on the phone," I said.

My mother came to the phone and said, "Hello, Gerald."

"Mom, I am at Steve's house. We are going to get started on the project now."

"Okay," she responded. "Gerald, I'll have your Dad pick you up when you are done."

"Okay, Mom, I love you."

"I love you, too, Gerald."

When I hung up the phone, Mrs. Miles called Steve. "Dinner is served, and I am leaving now."

"Gerald, would you like some dinner?" she asked.

"Yes, please."

"Please, come and have a seat."

When I came to the table, I saw barbecued chicken, corn on the cob, and mashed potatoes. After I said Grace, we were off to the races. I didn't have to worry about being greedy because both our faces were buried in our food. You couldn't find a crumb on either of our plates when we were finished. After we gulped down some soda, we took our plates to the sink. Steve put his plate in the sink and told me to follow him upstairs to his room.

"Steve, are you going to wash the plates?"

"No, Mrs. Miles does that."

I gazed at him with a puzzled look on my face. "I don't mind, I will wash and you rinse."

Steve hesitated at first but came back to the sink. When we had almost finished, he started splashing water on me. He got water on my face and started laughing. I had to get him back so I threw soapsuds and one landed on his nose. He retaliated by getting me on the forehead. We were going back and forth relentlessly. We finally stopped when we realized how wet the floor was. We got on our hands and knees with paper towels and dried up the floor.

While we were on the floor, Steve asked, "Hey, Gerald. Do you have any brothers and sisters?"

"I have one brother named Tyrone, and he is seven years old. I also have a sister named Tonya, and she is six years old."

"I don't have any brothers or sisters. It's just me."

"Having them is a lot of fun. I love my brother and sister. You'll get to meet them some day."

"That sounds cool."

After we made sure that the floor was completely dry, I followed Steve. When we reached the bottom of the staircase, I noticed how different it was. The house actually had a split staircase. There was one staircase on the right and one on the left. Both staircases met at the top.

Steve said, "I'll race you to the top. I'll start on the left side, and you can start on the right side."

I positioned myself at the bottom of the staircase. Steve was also ready and said, "On your mark, get set, go."

I started running up the stairs as fast as I could. I got halfway up before I stumbled. I wasn't too familiar with the stairs and that's all the advantage Steve needed.

He reached the top first and screamed, "I beat you! I beat you!"

When I looked around and saw how big the second floor was, I just stood paralyzed in amazement. The upstairs was humongous. I looked down at my feet and gazed at the wooden floors. They shined so brightly that I saw my own reflection. There were so many closed doors. It reminded me of a hotel. Steve's house looked like a maze.

He noticed that I was mesmerized and said, "Do you want the grand tour of the upstairs?"

"Sure, that's cool with me."

"We have seven bedrooms up here."

The first door we entered was at the end of the hallway on the right. This room contained five different computers and had all kinds of computer books sitting on the shelves. This room even had a bed and a television. Steve explained that was his mother's workroom, and that she sat in there for hours creating new computer programs.

The next room we entered was his father's room. The first things I saw were the bar and the pool table. This room was spacious. It had a big-screen television and a couple of leather couches. Steve explained this was where his father entertained clients and friends when he was at home.

The next room we entered was smaller than the first two. Steve explained this was a guest room for friends and family. The next room was a smaller guest room.

We entered Steve's playroom next. The first thing that caught my attention was the big-screen television. He also had video game systems, a computer, a ping-pong table, encyclopedias, and a couch. Steve told me he spent time in there when he was bored.

The next room on the far left-hand side of the hallway was Steve's parents' room. When we went inside, I saw how beautifully decorated it was. It had a king-sized bed, two televisions, a mini bar and a Jacuzzi. Their room basically took up that entire side of the house.

The last room we entered was Steve's bedroom. It had a king-sized bed, and Steve had all kinds of posters on the walls. Everything in his room was neatly arranged. Each room on the second floor had its own bathroom.

"Where's your closet?"

Steve pointed toward a door, which looked too small to put

all of his clothing in. When he opened it, I blinked a couple of times to make sure that I was seeing correctly. Steve had a huge walk-in closet—the size of my bedroom. Steve had sneakers, shoes, pants, shorts, and shirts organized neatly. He had enough clothing to go months without repeating the same thing. It was unbelievable; I stood there feeling jealous. But what fascinated me the most was that everything was color coordinated. For instance, he had a rack of blue clothes: pants, shirts, shorts, socks, underwear, hats, and sneakers. After Steve and I came out of his closet, I looked at my watch. It was almost eight o'clock.

"Wow, look at the time! May I please use your phone?"

"Sure man, it's by my bed."

When the phone call went through, my father answered.

"Hello, Dad. Can you please pick me up?"

"Sure, son, what is the address?"

I handed Steve the phone, and he gave my father the directions. I turned to Steve and said, "Sorry, man, but it's getting late. We'll have to start the science project another day. I'll come over another time."

We sat on his bed and laughed and horsed around. I began realizing that Steve was much cooler than I had previously thought. I actually enjoyed being around him. Thirty minutes later, the doorbell rang, and we went down to the front door. I opened the door and introduced Steve to my father. Afterwards, I put on my sneakers and told him I'd see him in school tomorrow.

While we were driving home, I began telling my father about Steve's house and what was in each room. I became really animated as I talked about Steve's closet and all his clothes. But my father gave me his infamous look, which meant that he had heard enough. I knew I had better stay quiet for the rest of the ride home.

My father turned the radio on to his oldies station. He listened to that station every time he got in the car. They happened to be playing Dad's favorite song. If I hadn't heard that song a hundred times, I hadn't heard it once. Every time it came on, my father turned up the volume. All I saw were his teeth as he smiled and sang along. It was some song from the 1960s. By repetition, I began singing the words in my head. I was careful that my father didn't see my lips move. If I admitted to my father that his music wasn't that bad, I knew I would have to listen to his music every time I got in the car.

We pulled up to the house, got out of the car, and went inside. I hugged my father then made my way into the living room. My mother was sitting on the couch reading the newspaper. I went over to her, gave her a hug, and went upstairs. I peeked into Tyrone and Tonya's room and saw that they were okay.

Tyrone must have been extremely tired, because he was snoring like an old man. I carefully closed their door and went into my room. I was exhausted; it had been a very long day, and I fell asleep in no time.

I woke up as my alarm clock started going off again. I jumped up and went through my daily routine. It was Wednesday and the third day of school. The only thing I was interested in was the upcoming weekend. I left my house and headed for the bus stop.

When I arrived at the bus stop, the line was long, but I waited patiently. Shortly afterwards, the bus arrived and everyone began boarding. When I got on the bus, someone from the back of the bus said, "Gerald, I saved a seat for you."

When I looked toward the back, I saw it was Suzanne. I became really nervous, and my heart began racing like a sports car. I made my way through the maze of people. When I reached the back of the bus, Suzanne smiled and removed her book bag from the seat she was saving for me. I felt a little funny because I didn't like what I wore. I sat down, and I was surrounded by a couple of her friends. They looked familiar, but I couldn't remember where I had seen them before. They looked me up and down and didn't say a word.

Suzanne watched as they stared at my clothes. "Girls, this is Gerald."

"Hello, Gerald."

"Hi, ladies."

Suzanne explained to them that I was new in school. As I looked at them again, I remembered where I'd seen them before. They were the girls who had spoken to Steve the day before.

One of the girls recognized me and said, "Aren't you one of the boys who was sitting at Steve's table?"

They all blushed, except for Suzanne who seemed uninterested. Another girl commented, "Steve is the man. He is such a cutie, and he looks jiggy every day. Does he have a girlfriend?"

I responded, "I don't know. You'll have to ask him yourself."

At that very moment, I felt like my father, and I wished they hadn't mentioned the word jiggy. When I looked at them, I noticed how jiggy they were dressed. Once again, I was an outsider in a private club. I was relieved when Suzanne's friends got off that subject and got lost in their own gossip.

Suzanne turned to me and started a conversation. "So, Gerald, where do you live?"

"On Elm Street."

"Okay, that's not too far from me," Suzanne said. "I live on

Oak Street. Do you have any brothers or sisters?"

"Yes, I have one brother and one sister. How about you?"

"I also have one brother and one sister."

As Suzanne talked, I focused all my attention on her. She had on a blue skirt, a white T-shirt, black sandals, and a blue ribbon in her hair. She was a vision of perfection. I felt so good being around her that I didn't want to get off the bus.

When our stop came, I rang the bell, and everyone who went to my school got off. I walked with Suzanne while her friends walked ahead of us. They were still gossiping about something so they weren't paying us any mind. I was really enjoying talking with Suzanne.

As we walked up the stairs to the entrance of the school, she asked, "Gerald, do you want to eat lunch with me today?"

I was so happy that I wanted to jump up and down. I took a deep breath to calm myself down. I wanted to be as cool as possible. "Sure. See you at lunchtime."

As I made my way to my homeroom, I heard voices. "Yo, Gerald, wait up!"

When I looked around, it was John and Bill. "What's up, fellows?"

John said, "Nothing. We saw you talking to Suzanne."

"Yeah. So what?"

Bill said, "Man, she is one of the cutest girls in the school."

John interrupted. "You're the luckiest guy in school."

Bill whispered in my ear, "Did you know she is the only girl in school that ever said 'no' to Steve when he asked her to go to lunch with him?"

I was shocked. "No way!"

"I'm serious," Bill said. "She wasn't interested."

That surprised me; Steve was the most popular boy in the whole school. I didn't think any girl would have rejected him. When we reached homeroom, I made my way to the back of the classroom and sat down. Steve was already seated. I gave him the universal nod, and he gave me the same. When I looked at Steve's feet, I noticed he was wearing the sneakers and the matching outfit he bought yesterday.

His bag was sitting in front of me, and I noticed something scribbled with a magic marker. When I stared a little closer, it said, "Mr. Jiggy Man."

The bell rang, and I went to my next class. All my classes were moving quickly. I actually wasn't paying much attention in any of them. The only thing on my mind was Suzanne and eating lunch with her. Before I realized, it was lunchtime, and I made my way toward the cafeteria. As I walked up to the entrance, I saw Suzanne waiting patiently.

As I approached, she had a big smile on her face. "Hi, Gerald."

I returned her smile and responded, "Hi, Suzanne."

We made our way into the lunchroom and got our lunches. After we paid for lunch, we found an empty table and sat together. I was enjoying being with her so much that I wanted the lunch period to go on forever. I was extremely disappointed when the bell rang. When I looked at my watch, I realized lunchtime was unfortunately over. At that point, I remembered what my father always said: "Time flies when you're having fun."

Suzanne and I walked to gym class. When I got to the locker room, I started getting excited. My day was going great, and, to top it off, I was in gym class. I got dressed and entered the gym. After Mrs. Julian finished attendance, she said, "Today, class, you can play basketball, volleyball, or badminton."

I instantly had a flashback as I looked at everyone in my gym class. Gym classes in my old school would never have been run like that. Boys and girls never played in the same gym period. The faculty had tried that before but decided it would be better if we were separated. I liked my new school's policy much better. Mrs. Julian had warned us on the first day of class that any unruly behavior was unacceptable. She was in complete control at all times.

Everyone in gym class began playing the activity they liked most. Bill and a couple of guys wanted to play a full court game of basketball. I became excited. This is what I had been waiting for from day one.

Anyone who wanted to play basketball began lining up in front of the free throw line. I was the tenth person on the line.

Before we began shooting, Mrs. Julian came over to the basketball courts. "Students, the rules are very simple. The first five who make a free throw are on the same team. The next five are on the opposing team. Have fun and play fair."

I watched as five people in a row made their free throws. After a couple of misses, it was my turn to shoot. I bounced the ball a couple of times and bent my knees and shot. It felt good as it rolled off my fingertips. The ball went through the net and made a swishing sound. I confidently said, "That's one for the other team."

There was a long line of students waiting for their turn. This was a fair practice, and I wished they did that in my old neighborhood. It was hard to get a game. The rules were extremely different. They would let the first two people who made the free throw be captains and they each picked four other people. The older guys never picked me. On many occasions, I didn't even get to shoot because the two free throws had already been made. I usually went to the other side of the park and played by myself.

We had four guys on our team, and the other team already

had five. There were ten more people waiting in line to shoot, including Suzanne. I wondered what she was doing in the line. Nine students came up to the line and missed. Suzanne was next, and she calmly walked up to the free throw line. She took her time, dribbled, bent her knees, and shot the basketball. She confidently left her hand in the shooting position as she watched the ball go through the net.

Girls never came to any park I played in, and none would dare to get on the court with the boys. The teams were finalized, and Suzanne was on mine. We got the ball first, and the game started.

Suzanne walked over to me and confidently said, "I'll play the point guard."

Point guard! That's my position. I wanted to tell her, "No way," but I kept that comment to myself.

On the first play, she dribbled around three defenders and put it through one of our opponents' legs before making a lay-up. Suzanne really knew how to ball. I never expected that she could be so good. She was better than most boys in our gym class. Play after play, she did something more spectacular than the previous one. She dribbled the ball, passed, and shot with little effort. She even hit me in the head with the ball once because I wasn't expecting her pass.

Our team won three games in a row, and Suzanne played the

biggest role in our victories. As the bell rang, I walked with her to the locker rooms and asked, "Where did you learn how to play like that?"

"My father. We spend a lot of time together."

I was definitely impressed. I went into the boys' locker, showered, and got dressed. I made my way through the hallway to my next class, which was science.

After attendance, Mr. Phillips asked, "How is everyone's project going? You guys have until Monday to give me an outline stating what your project will be."

When Mr. Phillips was writing on the board, someone handed me a folded piece of paper. When I opened it, I saw it was from Steve. It said, "Gerald, we'd better get some work done. Can I spend the weekend at your house?"

I was shocked. I couldn't figure out why Steve wanted to spend the weekend at my house when he had such a beautiful home. I wrote back and said, "I have to ask my parents first, but I don't think that will be a problem."

The rest of the day flew by, and I fell asleep on the bus and almost missed my stop. When I got home, I went straight upstairs. I was able to complete all my homework assignments without being interrupted. After homework, I was tired and decided to lie down.

I woke up when Tyrone began jumping on my bed. "Wake

up, Gerald. Gerald, wake up. Mommy's calling you," he screamed.

I went downstairs and went into the kitchen. My mother was at the stove. "Honey, get the drinks and plates," she instructed.

I was still half asleep, but when I smelled the food, I became wide-awake. I placed the plates and drinks on the table and called everyone to dinner. My mother brought lasagna to the table. I could already taste the lasagna on my tongue.

It was Tyrone's turn for Grace. Tyrone began speaking with a smile on his face. "Thank you, Lord, for Mommy and Daddy, Gerald and Tonya, and the food. And could you send me a puppy?"

Everyone chuckled and said, "Amen."

I ate like a man possessed. After the table was cleared, my mother came out with my favorite dessert, gelatin with fruit and vanilla ice cream. Tyrone and Tonya began clapping as my mother put it in their bowls. My father looked tired, so I said, "Dad, when we're finished, I'll wash the dishes."

"Thanks, son. I had a long day, and my back is killing me."

My mother interrupted. "Honey, do you want a massage?"

"Would you? That would be nice."

That was the thing I loved about my family. We always helped each other. I said to my mother, "Mommy, when I finish the dishes, I'll check Tyrone and Tonya's homework, and I'll have them wash up and put them to bed."

I went to the kitchen and quickly washed the dishes. Afterwards, I checked Tyrone and Tonya's homework. This was a very easy task because Tyrone and Tonya were smart. They were way ahead of their classmates. My parents spent a lot of time teaching them different things.

Fifteen minutes later, they were washed up and ready for bed. They wouldn't let me leave until I read them a bedtime story. They both fell asleep before the story ended. I left their room quietly, and I knocked on my parents' door.

"Come in," my mother said.

When I entered, I saw my mother looking through some papers and my father reading a magazine. "Could I talk to you guys for a minute?" I asked.

My father answered, "Sure, son. What's on your mind?"

"I am working on this science project with Steve. I was wondering if he could spend the weekend?"

"Sure, son."

"Thanks, Dad."

"Any time, son."

My mother interrupted. "Did you finish your homework?"

"Yes, mother."

"Okay. It's getting late, Gerald. You'd better get some sleep."

"Good night, Mom and Dad."

I went into my room, but I had a hard time falling asleep. I tossed and turned for half of the night. I eventually dozed off about midnight.

I awoke that next morning because someone was banging on my door. My mother entered my room. "Gerald, do you see the time? You're going to be late."

I looked at the clock, and it was fifteen minutes past eight. I jumped straight out of bed and stared at my clock again. I was really angry because I had forgotten to set my alarm clock last night. I ran into the bathroom, quickly showered, and brushed my teeth. I went back into my room, grabbed some clothes in my closet, and ran downstairs to the basement and ironed them. On my way up, I peeked in the kitchen and saw my father drinking his coffee. "Dad, can you give me a ride this morning?"

"Sure, son. By the way, can you get my toolbox in the basement?"

When I went downstairs, I almost tripped on my brother's toy car. I wondered what was in the toolbox because it was really heavy. My father was outside starting the car. Since I was running late, everyone was ready except for me. My mother sat in the front, and Tyrone, Tonya, and I sat in the back. I started thinking about how I blew my chance of seeing Suzanne at the bus stop. My father turned on the radio to his oldies station, and I thought, *not that station again!*

I was the first person he dropped off. I told everyone, "Bye," and I hopped out of the car and ran up the stairs. When I entered school, I noticed I was the only one in the hallway. I looked at my watch and realized I was late. When I entered the classroom, Mrs. Dixon was calling my name. I answered, "Present, Mrs. Dixon."

As I made my way to the back, I noticed Steve's desk was empty. I sat down and asked John and Bill, "Where's Steve?"

"I don't know. He didn't come in," John responded.

After homeroom was finished, I went into the hallway and saw Suzanne standing by her locker. She smiled and said, "Hi, Gerald."

"Hi, Suzanne."

"How come I didn't see you at the bus stop this morning?"

"I woke up late this morning."

"Well, do you want to eat lunch with me?"

"Sure. See you at lunchtime."

When I walked around the corner, I saw John and Bill looking at that flyer again. I was curious about what was on it and started walking toward them. Before I reached them, the bell rang, and they placed it back in Bill's book bag.

I quickly hurried to my next class. After class, I saw John and Bill in the hallway. I said, "Do you think we should call Steve's house to see if everything is okay?"

"That's a good idea," John responded.

Bill gave me Steve's telephone number, and we called. The phone must have rung twenty times before the maid answered.

"Hello. How can I help you?" Mrs. Miles said.

"Hello, Mrs. Miles, it's Gerald. Is Steve there?"

"Steve is upstairs sleeping," she replied.

"Is he okay?"

"He's fine. Steve suffers from migraine headaches from time to time. He just needs to get some rest."

"Well, tell him I hope he feels better. If he wakes up later, can you give him my phone number so he can call me?"

When I got off the phone, I told John and Bill what Mrs. Miles had said, and I headed to the cafeteria. Just as yesterday, Suzanne was waiting for me in front. We got our lunches and sat at an empty table. When I looked at Bill and John, they had sad, puppy-dog faces. They were completely lost without Steve. They sat at the table not saying too much to one another. I felt sorry for them, but my full attention was on Suzanne. As soon as we started a conversation, her friends came to our table and sat down.

Suzanne said, "Hey, girls, would you mind if Gerald and I sat alone? We'll hang out later."

They gave me a funny look and said, "Okay, Suzanne, see you after school."

That made me feel very special. I felt honored to be sitting with Suzanne. When I looked around, I noticed students were staring at us, and some were whispering. Gossip was a big thing in my school, and I knew the topic was about Suzanne and me.

I bent down and started adjusting my pants cuff because it looked a little crooked. As I looked under the table, I noticed Suzanne's notebook had fallen out of her bag.

As I was returning her notebook, a couple of her papers fell out. I felt like such a klutz, and I began picking them up. One of the papers I retrieved looked very familiar. I looked again and realized that it was that flyer that everyone had been looking at. That was the closest I had ever been to it. As I handed it back to her, I asked, "What's on that flyer?"

"Every year, WXYZ 91.0 runs a contest only for our school. The contest rewards students who can name any song they describe. You have to know the song, the artist, and the year it was recorded."

"Wow! That seems like a lot of fun. So what do you win?"

"You win $5,000."

I stuttered and said, "Fi- fi- five thousand dollars! Are you serious? What kind of music?"

"All kinds of music. Anything from opera to reggae."

"So it must be hard to win?"

"Who are you telling? No one has won this contest in three years."

I couldn't believe it. "Three years."

"Yes, three years. Everyone has been really secretive about it because everyone wants to win. But I heard through the grapevine that this year's category of music is going to be hip-hop."

Suzanne took a sip of her juice and continued, "The whole school knows by now. Students have already begun forming study groups. They quiz one another on songs and stuff, but when the contest begins it's every man for himself. It will be announced in homeroom on Friday over the loud speaker. But first you have to pass the first phase."

I was confused. "The first phase?"

"Yeah! Anyone interested has to go to the gym after school. But this is where it gets hard. Whoever wants a chance at winning the money has to sink a basket from the free throw line with their opposite hand."

"What do you mean?"

"If you're left-handed, you have to make it with your right, and if you're right-handed, you have to make it with your left."

"That sounds very hard."

During the whole conversation, I kept looking over at John and Bill. No one approached their table. But when Steve was around, it was as busy as a flea market on a Saturday morning.

The bell rang, and I told Suzanne goodbye and caught up with John and Bill in the hallway. "What's up? Are you guys entering the music contest?"

They looked shocked and didn't respond.

"How come you guys didn't tell me about the contest?"

John answered, "My fault. It kind of slipped my mind."

Bill said, "I guess you don't have to worry about making the first cut. You're a good basketball player."

I was really upset because they hadn't told me about the contest. "So what? It's one shot. Anyone can make it or miss it."

Our conversation was cut short when the bell rang. I headed to gym class. When I entered, Mrs. Julian took attendance. She gave us the same choices of activities as yesterday. But no one was playing volleyball or badminton. Every hoop in the gym was occupied. The whole class was shooting free throws with their opposite hands. I decided to shoot, too, because I was not used to shooting a free throw with my opposite hand. I was really pitiful. I went up to the line time after time and missed. I was becoming frustrated because, on more than a few occasions, I didn't even hit the rim. I felt relieved when the bell rang. I got showered and dressed in the locker room and went to my next class.

After class, I stayed in my seat for homeroom, which was noisier than usual. I listened closely as students quizzed one another on hip-hop songs. It seemed like the whole school was preparing for the contest. After homeroom was finished, I walked to the bus stop. Ten minutes later the bus came. While I sat in my seat, I thought, "What if I'm the one to win the contest? Five thousand dollars! Man, what a lot of money! I could buy all the clothes I want to. I could be jiggy for the rest of the year!"

Every student from our school who was on the bus was talking about the contest and hoping they would make the free throw. I listened as two people got into a heated argument about an artist for a hip-hop song.

I decided to look out the window. As I looked, I saw that billboard that Steve was talking about. I jumped up and rang the bell and got off the bus. I walked down the block and headed toward Mr. Smith's store.

When I entered the store, I saw Mr. Smith.

"Hello, young man. You look familiar. Have I seen you in this store recently?"

"Yes, sir, I was with Steve."

"Okay, how can I help you?"

"I am just looking for now."

I felt like a kid in a candy store. I looked at sneakers and even tried on a couple of pairs. After that I tried on pants, sweat suits, hats, shirts, and T-shirts. I must have tried on twenty different items. I looked at my watch and realized it was getting late. I said to Mr. Smith, "Thanks. Maybe I'll buy something another time."

"Okay, young man. I'll be here when you're ready."

When I reached home, I went straight upstairs and got into bed. I wasn't hungry because all my thoughts were focused on the contest. I made sure that I set my alarm clock because I wanted to see Suzanne in the morning.

My alarm clock went off, and I woke up with a terrible headache. It was Friday and my fifth day of school. I wanted to stay in bed that morning. I sat and thought about the very interesting dream I had last night. It had seemed so real. I had dreamt that I was the winner of the contest.

I remembered answering the $5,000 question with the greatest of ease. Afterwards, several banners came streaming down onto the gym floor, and I was declared the winner. I was presented with a check for $5,000, and the local newspapers were taking my picture. Everyone in school was congratulating me, and after my quick interview with the radio station, I was rushed away in a limo.

The limo was hot! It had a TV, a VCR, a DVD, a mini-bar, a telephone, and a computer. Suzanne was sitting by my side. She was looking good. She gave me a big kiss on the cheek and said, "Gerald, you're the man."

The limo driver asked, "Where to, sir?"

"To Mr. Smith's store on Wood Street."

After I entered Mr. Smith's store, he said, "Hello, Gerald, I heard you won the contest. How can I help you?"

"Mr. Smith, give me one of everything."

I searched through all his merchandise. I even bought a couple of outfits for Suzanne. After I finished picking out the things I wanted, I went straight up to the register. I took out the check and handed it to Mr. Smith. I spent every dime in his store and went back to the limo. I dropped Suzanne off at her house, and she gave me a big hug and kissed me on the cheek again. The next day at school, I was a celebrity. Students who didn't know me wanted to be my friend. I was the new Mr. Jiggy Man for the rest of the year. That is what everyone called me. I had my own lunch table, and on it was a sign that said, "Seating for Mr. Jiggy Man."

Steve was still jiggy, but I was just as jiggy as he was. But since I was the new attraction and had been on TV and in the newspapers, I was the most popular person in school.

Man, what a dream!

I went through my morning routine and left my house. I looked for Suzanne at the bus stop, but she wasn't there. There was no reason for me to be up, so I just slept as we drove along. When I got off the bus, I closed my eyes for a minute. I wished my dream had been reality and that I had won the money.

When I entered homeroom, everyone seemed extremely excited. First, it was Friday, and second, it was the first phase of the contest. John, Bill, and a group of others were passing around this sheet with hip-hop songs, artists, titles, and years recorded. This list had some songs dating as far back as ten years ago. I asked Bill, "Where did you get this from?"

"From Ted, who sits up in the front. He's a real geek. We promised if he gave the list to us, we would let him sit with us at the lunch table."

I asked curiously, "Isn't he going to enter the contest?"

John laughed. "Ted! Yeah, right. He can't even dribble a basketball, let alone make a shot with his opposite hand. Ted knows he doesn't have a chance, so we struck a deal with him."

I said, "You never know. He could get lucky."

John responded, "Could be, but you know what? Geeks know

their limitations, and they don't like looking stupid. Ted won't embarrass himself by trying."

I realized this contest was getting really competitive. Some students were studying the sheet more than they studied their schoolwork. Everyone had different thoughts on what they would do with the money. But I knew that most people wanted to use the money to impress others. Well, I was guilty as well because that's what I planned to do.

Steve wasn't sitting in front of me, and I wondered if he was coming to school. The class quieted down as Mrs. Dixon started calling attendance. When she called Steve's name, he hurried through the door. "Present, Mrs. Dixon!"

Steve turned around and said, "Hey, Gerald, what's up?"

"Nothing. Are you entering the contest today?"

"Of course! I have a lot of ideas on what I could do with that money."

"What?"

"It's a secret. You'll know when I win."

Bill and John passed Steve a sheet, and he studied it intensely before the bell rang. I wondered what he would use the money for. He had everything a kid could want.

When homeroom ended, I went into the hallway and saw everyone was focused on their sheets. When a teacher passed by, they would put them away so they wouldn't get caught.

I saw Suzanne in the hallway and approached her. "Hi, Suzanne."

"Hi, Gerald."

"I didn't see you at the bus stop this morning."

"I got a ride today. Did you miss me?"

I blushed and said, "Yeah, I did."

Suzanne smiled and said, "See you at lunch later?"

I headed quickly to my next class. In every class I went to, I saw the same thing. Everyone was studying the sheets while the teacher wrote notes on the blackboard. I wasn't about to try that, so I copied all my teachers' notes down and paid attention. I was a straight "A" student in my old school. If my grades slipped, my parents would kill me. I decided it was better if I looked at the sheets at lunchtime when I wouldn't be interrupted. All my classes breezed by. When I went to science class, the teacher reminded us that the outlines for our projects were due next week.

I passed a note to Steve telling him that my parents didn't mind if he slept over on the weekend. Steve wrote back indicating that he had already spoken to his parents about spending the weekend.

The bell rang, and I went to lunch. Like the past two days, Suzanne waited patiently in front of the cafeteria. We walked in together. John, Bill, and Steve were sitting at their table.

After I got my lunch, I walked by their table. John and Bill gave me the thumbs up, which meant that they approved of Suzanne. I winked back at them when she wasn't looking. I felt good because she was cute, athletic, intelligent, and, to top it off, I was the only one sitting with her. We sat down, and she took out her sheet and gave me a copy. I looked over it for about ten minutes, but I was getting bored.

Suzanne saw me put it away and asked, "Why aren't you studying?"

"It's boring."

"Well, I want to win. Don't you?"

"Of course I do. What would you do with the money if you won?"

"I would use some money to make flyers to start a clothing drive for the school. A lot of people don't have clothes for the winter. I would also like to create a Big Brother and Big Sister Club, where students would pair up with other kids and do things together. Not everyone has the luxury of knowing their family. If people feel lonely, they can pair up with someone else. I would schedule trips, and all the big brothers and big sisters would go together. I also would like a new computer. And if I had any money left over, I would do some clothes shopping for myself."

I was impressed and said, "Wow! You have big plans."

I got up and emptied my tray. On my way back, I sat down at the table with Bill, John, and Steve. They were all studying their sheets. One of Suzanne's friends walked past the table, smiled, and said, "Hi, Steve. We missed you yesterday."

"I didn't feel well."

She rubbed his head and said, "You look cute today. Nice shirt."

"Thanks."

It was amazing how Steve benefited from being jiggy. He always got a lot of attention. That was the life I wanted to live. What more could a person ask for? The fellows weren't paying much attention to me because their heads were buried in the sheets. I got up and went back over to Suzanne. We talked and joked about the first time I attempted to play badminton.

The bell rang, and I walked with Suzanne toward the locker rooms. After I got dressed, I walked into gym class. Mrs. Julian took attendance and announced, "Class, I noticed everyone was practicing yesterday for this contest, so the only activity today will be shooting baskets."

Mrs. Julian went to the back and came out with a rack of basketballs. Everyone lined up behind free throw lines as we had done yesterday. There were eight basketball hoops to shoot at. Suzanne and I were on the same line. I took a lot of shots but failed to make any baskets. I got a little worried because I would only have one chance after school. Bill and John were practicing, and Bill made three in a row. I looked across the gym and saw Ted practicing all by himself. He was working up a sweat, and his friends known as the Geek Pack were giving him instructions on how to make the basket.

"Ted, move a little to the left," one said.

Another said, "Bend your knees."

The bell rang; after I got showered and dressed, I went to English class. English class ended quickly, and I sat in the same seat for homeroom. Mrs. Dixon asked for the class's attention and said, "Class, good luck to those who are trying to make the free throw today. I hope at least one person from this homeroom makes it."

All of a sudden, we heard microphone feedback coming from the loudspeaker. It was the assistant principal, and he told the whole school that the contest would be held in the gym after homeroom. I was really pumped up, but at the same time really nervous. The bell rang, and everyone in homeroom gathered their belongings. The hallway was extremely crowded because a lot of students were heading toward the gym. As I looked in front of me, Ted was also heading in the direction of the gym. Ted had a determined look on his face. John, Bill, and Steve were a little farther ahead of me.

When I entered the gym, I saw hundreds of students in line.

Everyone who entered signed an attendance sheet. We sat in the bleachers and waited until our names were called. There was one basketball in front of each of the eight hoops. Wildman Bill from WXYZ 91.0 on the FM dial took the microphone. "Hello, boys and girls. How are you today?"

Everyone answered back, "Fine, Wildman Bill!"

Wildman Bill said, "Is anyone ready to win $5,000? Make some noise!"

Students began stomping their feet and clapping their hands. It felt like I was at a professional basketball game. We all listened carefully as Wildman Bill's assistants called the names. This became a long process, and I was getting bored sitting around. Finally, after two hours, my name was called, and I was on line with about forty other kids. I looked over at the other lines and noticed John, Bill, and Steve were on the same line. Ted and Suzanne were together in another line.

There were so many faces I had never seen before. The Junior Varsity basketball team was also out in full force. They wore their personalized leather jackets with "JV" and their nicknames written on the back. They were all joking around as they stood together.

Wildman Bill took the microphone. "Let the games begin!"

I was the last one on my line, so I knew it would be a long time before I got to shoot. The pressure started getting to me, and I started becoming really nervous. I focused my attention on others so I wouldn't think about myself. I looked over at Suzanne's line, and she was the first in line. I watched as she calmly went up to the free throw line and sank the basket. She jumped up and down, pumping her fist in the air. She ran off the line, grabbed her backpack from the bleachers, and left the gym.

On the other side of the gym, I watched as John made his basket. Bill came up to the free throw line and made his basket. Afterwards, Steve came up to the free throw line and made his basket. I felt pressured. I was the only one out of the crew who hadn't made the basket. I looked from line to line. I watched as students came up to the line, time and time again missing the free throw. Quite a few kids slammed the ball down after they missed their shots.

I focused my attention on my line and saw that there were five people left. It would only be a couple of minutes before I shot the ball. I looked back at the line where Suzanne had been standing, and I saw Ted go up. One of Wildman Bill's assistants threw him the ball, and it hit him in the face. Ted's glasses flew off his face, and several kids in the gym started laughing. He ran over to his glasses and picked them up. He took a handkerchief out of his pocket, cleaned them off carefully, and returned back to the free throw line. He bounced the ball three times really hard and stood there with the ball in a shooting position. I saw the concentration on his face; sweat ran down his forehead. He bent his knees then shot the ball. The ball hit the front end of the rim, bounced really high in the air then came straight down right through the net.

Ted screamed, "YES! YES! YES! I did it! I did it!"

Everyone was surprised because Ted never played basketball in gym class. I guessed the basketball gods were watching over him. He ran to the bleachers, grabbed his backpack, and made his way to the exit. His friends were standing at the exit and started chanting, "TEDDY! TEDDY! TEDDY!"

I looked up at the bleachers and saw that John, Bill, and Steve were waiting for me. I focused my attention back on my line and saw I was the next one up. I must have dribbled the ball twenty times before I shot it. I bent my knees, focused on the rim, and shot the ball. The ball hit the rim and rolled around three times before it went through. I felt as if a 400-pound weight had been lifted from my shoulders.

I was so happy! I had made it past the first cut. I ran up the bleachers and John, Bill, and Steve gave me high fives. We all survived the first cut.

Wildman Bill came to the microphone and announced, "Congratulations to all who made it to the second round. See everyone next week when I ask the $5,000 question. This is

Wildman Bill from WXYZ 91.0 signing off. OW! OW! OW! OW! OW! OW."

Everyone imitated Wildman Bill's wolf call. "OW! OW! OW! OW! OW! OW! OW! OW!"

I was curious about how many students made the basket. I went up to one of Wildman Bill's assistants and asked. I was surprised. Out of 559 students, twenty-five people made it.

John, Bill, Steve, and I were excited as we walked to the bus stop. When we got to the bus stop line, I saw a lot of disappointed faces. No one from the JV team made the shot. Ted also stood at the bus stop, and all I saw were his braces as he smiled from ear to ear. The bus arrived and I sat next to Steve. John and Bill sat together. Steve told me that he was going to his house to get his things. I told him that would be okay, and I asked if I could tag along.

As we drove along, John and Bill studied their sheets until their stop came. They gave us the nod as they exited through the back door. Steve and I stayed on the bus until we reached his stop.

When we got to Steve's house, I sat in the living room while he went upstairs and got his clothes. I was totally relaxed on the leather couch. Fifteen minutes later, he came downstairs with a small suitcase. I wondered what that was for; he was only spending the weekend. But by the way he lugged the suitcase down the stairs, he appeared to have enough clothes for one week.

We left Steve's house and headed to the bus stop. One of his neighbors, who was washing his red convertible, called out, "Hi, Steve, how are your parents?"

"Fine."

"Are they out of town?"

"Yes."

"When will they get back?"

"I'm not sure. They're on work-related business."

"Who was that?" I asked.

"That was one of my father's friends. They hang out together when my father's in town."

I took another look at the red convertible, and I wondered how I would look behind the wheel. If I had that car, I would drive it all around town with the top down and the music blasting.

We waited about a half an hour for the bus. I was relieved when it arrived because my feet were aching. When we got to my stop, I rang the bell. Steve and I exited from the front of the bus and made our way up the block. We stopped briefly in front of the flower shop to speak with Max. Steve struggled as he dragged his suitcase down the block. I looked at my watch, and it was 5:30 p.m. I knew that everyone would be home.

When I got inside, Tyrone and Tonya ran to the door and both jumped on me.

Tyrone said, "Gerald's home! Gerald's home!"

"Gerald, who's your friend?" Tonya asked.

"Steve."

"Hi, Steve," Tonya said.

"I bet I can guess your name," Steve said.

"Go ahead. Try."

"Tonya."

"You can't trick me. Gerald told you."

Steve looked surprised. But I knew how observant Tyrone and Tonya were.

My little brother interrupted and said, "So you know my name is Tyrone."

Afterwards we went into the kitchen, and I introduced Steve to my mother. I took him upstairs and showed him to the guestroom. He put his suitcase inside, and we came back downstairs.

I heard my father calling my name, and Steve and I went to the backyard. My father was hard at work building a deck at the back portion of our house. He had his dust mask on while he was sawing a piece of wood.

Steve stared as my father toiled away. "That looks like hard work, Mr. Henderson."

"It's okay once you get the hang of it. Steve, would you like to help?"

"I've never worked with my hands before."

"Well, there is a first time for everything." He looked at me and said, "Gerald, go downstairs and get Steve an apron and get one for yourself. You guys can help me before dinner."

I went inside, got two aprons, and sprinted back to the backyard. I handed Steve his apron, and we put them on and looked at my father for instructions.

My father asked, "Steve, have you ever used a hammer before?"

"No, sir."

My father handed Steve a hammer and told me to get one out of his toolbox. I loved helping my father. I got to spend a lot of quality time with him, and I learned valuable skills for the future. I had been helping my father for years, so I knew exactly how to use one.

My father said to Steve, "It is always good to know a little bit about everything. You may not know how to fix everything, but if you have an idea, no one can ever rip you off if something needs to be fixed."

My father readjusted his tool belt and said, "Gerald, Steve, get some nails and two measuring tapes out of my toolbox and come over here."

We quickly got them and awaited his next instructions. "Gerald, hammer the nails into the wood over to your left, seven inches apart."

"Okay Dad."

My father turned to Steve and said, "First you'll be using the measuring tape. Can you locate seven inches on it?"

Steve hesitantly responded, "Yes."

"Next, I want you to hammer in one nail every seven inches along the wood beam until you reach the end."

My father showed Steve how to hold a hammer and demonstrated how a nail was hammered in. "If you hit a nail and it is crooked, use the back end of the hammer and pull it out."

Steve started hammering away; after a couple of mistakes, he was going down the beam like a seasoned veteran. He had total concentration written all over his face. My father didn't stand over him. He gave Steve space to learn from his own mistakes.

My father continued sawing away. After we'd been hitting nails for thirty minutes, my mother came to the back and told us that dinner would be served in fifteen minutes. My father stopped sawing and inspected Steve's work. Steve looked on nervously as my father looked at each hole meticulously.

"Well done, Steve. That's perfect."

Steve smiled and looked relieved. "Thank you, Mr.

Henderson."

"You never know how well you can do something until you first try. Then you keep trying and trying and trying until you complete it."

We went inside, and Steve and I went upstairs to wash our hands.

"Gerald, your father is cool. He really taught me something, and I enjoyed it as well. It must be so much fun having him around every day."

"Yeah, it's a lot of fun. Let's go downstairs."

Tonya and Tyrone had already done their part of setting the table. I went to the kitchen and got the drinks and plates. Steve was behind me.

"Can I help?" he asked.

"Sure, man, take the plates."

I was completely shocked. This was the same person who never even washed dishes. We were seated, and my mother came out with meatloaf, vegetables, and mashed potatoes. The best part of the day was eating my mother's cooking.

It was my father's turn to say Grace, and he started, "God bless our home, family, and food, and bless our visitor, Steve."

Eating Mom's meatloaf was a treat. As I looked over at Steve's plate, I saw he enjoyed it as well. He and I went back for seconds. After we ate and the dishes were cleared, it was dessert time. A familiar smell came from the kitchen. When my mother returned, she brought out apple pie. My mother sure knew how to bake, and she made most pies from scratch.

Before we dug in, she went back in the kitchen and brought out ice cream. There were four different flavors: vanilla, chocolate, strawberry, and orange sherbet. I took one scoop of each.

It was delicious. Steve and I went back for thirds. After dessert, my parents went into the living room. Tyrone and Tonya were playing on the floor in the next room.

Steve said, "Hey, Gerald. I'll wash, and you rinse."

We washed the dishes then came into the living room. My mother and father were sitting on the couch, and we sat beside them. Steve thanked my mother for the dinner. He turned to my father and asked, "Mr. Henderson, how many years have you been a carpenter?"

"For thirteen years."

"Wow, Mr. Henderson! Could you teach me some more carpentry skills?"

"Sure, Steve. You're welcome to come over and learn anytime."

We got up and went into the den where Tonya and Tyrone were playing. My sister said to Steve, "Would you like to play cards with me?"

"Okay."

"We'll play Concentration," Tonya said. "You and I are on one team. Gerald and Tyrone are on the other team."

We played Concentration often because it strengthened Tyrone and Tonya's memory. Steve had never played Concentration before so I explained the rules to him. "Steve, we take a pack of cards, spread them out on the floor face down. When it's your turn, you pick two cards at a time. Make sure the cards you pick are face up so everyone can see them. If you turn two cards that are the same, you have a match. Then you can pick them up, and you go again. If they're not a match, you put them down and try to remember where you put them."

"I think I got it," Steve responded.

Tyrone and Tonya played all the time, and I really concentrated when I played with them. They felt really good when they beat me.

The game began. Tonya turned over two cards, I turned over two cards, Steve turned over two cards, and Tyrone turned over two cards. Tonya got on a roll and made seven pairs in a row, and Steve made four pairs in a row.

Steve and Tonya won three games, and Tyrone and I had only beaten them once. Every time Tonya won a game, she gave Steve a big hug.

Since Tonya and Steve won more games, Tyrone insisted we

switch teams because he hated to lose. When we switched, Tyrone and Steve won three games, and Tonya and I won one. Every time Steve and Tyrone won, they gave each other high fives. I could tell that Tyrone and Tonya really enjoyed being around Steve. He appeared to like being around them as well.

Tyrone and Tonya had loads of energy on Fridays because they knew they didn't have to go to school the next day. I looked at the time and told them it was time to go to bed. As we passed my parents, who were watching TV, I said, "I'm going upstairs, Mom and Dad. I'll put Tyrone and Tonya to bed."

Tyrone and Tonya said, "Good night, Mommy and Daddy."

I went with them into the bathroom and made sure they washed up. Steve went to his room. After Tyrone and Tonya finished, I took them to their room to put on their pajamas. When they got dressed, they made me take them to Steve's room. Tyrone knocked on the door.

"Come in," Steve said.

"Steve, can you PLEASE read us a bedtime story?" Tonya asked.

Steve looked honored and went to their room and started reading one about a young prince. I told Steve to knock on my door when he was finished. I was cleaning up my room when he knocked. "Come in," I said. "You're finished?"

"Yeah, they're sound asleep. You're lucky. I wish I had a brother and sister. What were you doing in here?"

"Nothing much, just cleaning up."

We sat up for a while talking, and Steve looked tired. I learned something new about him every time I was around him. He left my room and went into his own and closed his door. I was getting tired so I turned off my light and went to sleep.

I awoke the next morning to the sounds of laughter. I wanted to know who was making all that noise on a Saturday morning. I usually slept late because I didn't have school. When I checked my clock, it was seven in the morning. I got out of bed and went to Steve's room. But as I approached, I noticed his door was already opened. I peeked inside and saw the bed was made and he wasn't in sight. I went downstairs into the living room and saw Steve, Tyrone, and Tonya watching cartoons. Tonya and Tyrone were sitting on Steve's lap and having a good time.

I went into the kitchen and saw my mother preparing breakfast. I asked her where Dad was, and she told me that he was in the basement. I went downstairs and watched as my father gathered his tools to work outside. He worked on the

deck every chance he got. My father was determined to get it
finished. I came back upstairs and looked in the backyard. I
noticed the grass needed cutting. Cutting the grass was one of
my chores I loved doing.

I ran upstairs and put on some older clothes. I got dressed,
went to the garage, and got out the lawnmower. I started the
engine and began mowing the lawn. Steve came out back and
asked me if I needed some help. I told him that I would be
okay.

While I was mowing the lawn, my father came outside and
started sawing wood. I was out there for over an hour, as I
mowed, raked, and bagged the grass.

In my old neighborhood, I lived in an apartment building. I
called that place, "the city of concrete." The only grass you
saw was at the front of the building, and there was a sign
saying, "KEEP OFF THE GRASS," so no one walked on it.

The sun started coming out, and I lay on the grass staring up
at the clouds. Staring at the sky was a new thing for me. I had
been doing it ever since we moved into our new home. Steve,
Tyrone, and Tonya came outside and joined me on the grass.
By using our imaginations, clouds resembled everything from a
pillow to a baseball bat.

We were interrupted when my mother came outside and told
us that breakfast was served. We got up and went upstairs and

washed our hands. When we finished, we hurried to the table. My mother had already set the table, so everyone sat down. She came out with sausages, bacon, eggs, pancakes, and a fruit platter. It was my turn to say Grace, and I wanted to make it short and sweet. I hurriedly said, "Lord, bless the food and bless everyone sitting at the table. Amen." We dug in.

Afterwards, Steve and I went upstairs.

I figured it would be better if we worked on our science project later in the day. Steve got in the shower first. I went to my room and made my bed. I had no idea what Steve wanted to do before then, and I didn't want to stay in the house all day because it was such a beautiful day. I went downstairs, ironed my clothes, and tried to think of something that could pass the time. When I got back upstairs, Steve was finished and was in his room.

I got in the shower. Afterwards, I went to my room and turned on the radio. The DJ said that a new arcade with a bunch of new games was having a grand opening on the first floor of the mall. You could play all the games you wanted and lunch was included. They opened at eleven o'clock, and the first sixty people got in for free. I quickly put on my clothes and knocked on Steve's door. "Are you ready?" I asked.

"Hold on a minute. What's the rush?"

"If we hurry, we can get an all-day pass to the new arcade in the mall."

When Steve came out of the room, I just stared. He wore two colors: black and orange. He had on black jeans, an orange shirt-shirt, orange hat, black and orange wristwatch, and black sneakers with orange laces. My outfit looked whack next to Steve's. I had colors that didn't go together.

I grabbed my hat in my room and went outside and tried convincing my father that we needed a ride downtown. I begged for what seemed like eternity. He finally gave in and went to the front and warmed up the car.

When we all got inside, my father did something out of the ordinary. He turned the radio to WXYZ 91.0, the hip-hop station. As we traveled downtown, Steve and I were bopping our heads in unison to the music.

When we approached the mall entrance, I noticed there were already several people standing outside. As we got out, Steve and I sprinted to the line. Luckily, we got to the line just before two other people. One of them was tying his shoelaces, and the other one was waiting for him to finish.

The doors opened, and they began letting people in. Steve and I made numbers fifty-nine and sixty. The boy who waited for his friend to tie his shoelaces was really upset. He turned to him and said, "You should have tied your laces in the line."

When we entered the arcade, I was overwhelmed. I had only

seen those games in video game magazines. Steve and I were waiting patiently in the line for this one game called, "Warrior's Genesis." You were given gloves and had to stand directly on a glowing grid. This was a fighting game, and all the moves you did on the grid, you saw on the screen. The graphics were unbelievable, and we watched as someone playing before us demolished all newcomers. A few minutes later, a couple of girls walked by us, and they waved to Steve. One said, "Nice sneakers."

"Thank you," Steve replied.

None of those girls paid any attention to me. It really paid to be jiggy. Everyone wanted to be Steve's friend.

It was finally my turn, and I was enjoying myself. I won seven games in a row before a newcomer effortlessly finished me off. Steve went up next and only won once. The girls were clapping like he was doing well.

Afterwards, they came up to him and said, "You were fantastic! My name is Shelly, and that's Denise and Stacy."

"Hi, ladies! My name is Steve, and that's Gerald."

The first thing they did was look me up and down then they gave me a fake smile. I thought, *don't worry, if I ever win that contest everyone will want to talk to me and be my friend.*

I spent most of the time playing games, while Steve entertained his fans.

"What kind of shirt is that?" one of the girls asked.

Steve realized that I was becoming upset, so he took their phone numbers and told them goodbye. We went up to the second floor of the arcade. They had a very interesting game called "Escape from Destruction." The object of the game was to hit one another with these lasers, but you could hide anywhere. We had to put on this fluorescent suit and goggles and carry a laser gun.

I looked into the goggles, and everything was three-dimensional. There were so many places you could hide, and there were about thirty other kids in the room. If someone shot you, your suit beeped and you left the room. We spent a lot of time in this room and went back several times when we got hit.

My stomach began to growl, so I wanted to get something to eat. Since we had an all-day pass, we decided to hang out in the mall and return later. We went downstairs to Joe's Pizza and ordered two slices each and two Cokes. As we sat down and ate, the girls we met earlier walked by the pizza place and waved. Joe's Pizza was definitely good. I didn't leave any crumbs on my plate.

The mall downtown was huge. It had five floors, and you could definitely get lost in it. Every name brand of clothing and sneakers you ever heard of were there. We went into a sneaker store and bumped into John and Bill.

"What's up, guys?" I said.

"Yo, Gerald, Steve, what's up?" John said.

I asked, "What are you guys doing in here?"

"Buying sneakers," John said.

They were at the cash register paying for their sneakers. While John, Bill, and Steve were talking, I went over to the sneaker section. The sneakers they were purchasing were $95. That was expensive to me. I didn't have anything in my closet that was worth that much.

John and Bill followed us as we walked around the mall. Steve and I got bored and split up with them. We went back into the arcade and played some more games. We went over to a basketball game called, "Shooters Beware." The object of the game was to make as many baskets as you could in fifteen seconds. To win a prize, you had to make ten baskets. I figured that was easy enough. I watched as someone else played the game. The first five baskets were kind of close. The next thing I knew, the basket moved.

I shouted, "A moving basket! That's crazy."

The person playing missed the next twelve times. It looked like fun, so I decided to give it a shot. I really concentrated on the rim as I shot the ball and made my first five. The basket moved up, down, around, and sideways, but I managed to hit the next four. Steve cheered me on while I was shooting. I looked at the clock. I had made nine baskets, and I only had four seconds left. I grabbed a ball that came down to me, shot it, and it went in. Steve and I jumped up in the air. I went to the register with my ticket. They had all kinds of prizes. I looked carefully, and I spotted a huge teddy bear. It was almost the size of Tonya, and I knew how much she liked stuffed animals. I said, "Sir, give me that huge stuffed animal, please."

I turned to Steve and said, "Yo, why don't you give it a shot?"

"You know I'm not that good in basketball."

"So what? Concentrate. Remember the game we played at my house, Concentration. It's the same thing. If you concentrate, you can do it."

"I don't think so."

"You made the basket at gym yesterday."

"Yeah, I know, but that was luck."

"I don't think so. You did everything you were supposed to, and you took your time. Just give it a try. Don't you remember what my father told you?"

Steve paused and said, "Okay, you're right. You don't know until you try, and you should keep trying until you complete it."

That was all the encouragement Steve needed. He went up to the line and began shooting. Ten minutes later, he was still shooting. He had a determined look on his face, and I could tell he wasn't going to give up. He was concentrating very hard, and I heard him mumbling, "I can do it. I can do it."

On his fifth attempt, he made ten baskets. He proudly took the ticket to the cash register. As we walked, he said, "Thanks for helping me."

"No, Steve. Thank yourself for believing in yourself."

"You know what?"

"What?"

"What kind of toy does your brother like?"

"Action figures."

Steve looked through the selection of toys and saw an army soldier. He was bigger than most action figures and had several accessories. He had three different outfits and even a jeep, which he sat in. The soldier had moveable hands, legs, and arms. It came in a huge box, and Steve decided to get it.

It was three o'clock, and we decided we had had enough of the mall. We left and waited for the bus. It was a warm day, and I was sweating. I turned to Steve and said, "I wish we could go to the pool."

"Sure, we can," Steve responded. "Let's go to my house. I have a swimming pool in my backyard."

As we rode to Steve's house, all he talked about was how he made the ten baskets. When we reached his house, he went upstairs. "Gerald, I am going to get changed. I'll bring you down a pair of swimming trunks."

When he came down, he handed me a pair of swimming trunks. When I looked at the tag, I realized I was about to put on designer trunks. That was the latest fashion I had ever had on in my life. I wore those trunks like a soldier who just received a medal for his bravery.

We walked through his house and went into the backyard. And then I saw the swimming pool. It was huge; thirty kids could easily have fit into his pool. I was no stranger to water because I had been taking swimming lessons since I was a little kid. I walked up on the diving board and stared down into the water. I noticed that the deep end of the pool was separated with a rope from the shallow end. I jumped off the diving board and did a flip in the air and landed in the water. When I came up for air, I noticed Steve was sitting near the shallow end. "Hey, Steve, come in on the deep end."

Steve hesitated and said, "Nah. I better not. I can't swim. I'll stay in the shallow part."

I was surprised. He had a nice pool and he couldn't swim. "How come you can't swim?"

"My parents said they would show me, but they are never here. When they are here, they don't seem to have the time to teach me. I would love to learn though."

I swam to the shallow end and said, "Lesson one begins today."

"For real! You'll show me?" Steve said in an excited voice.

"Of course, I will."

"All right, what do I do?"

"Well, first you learn how to kick." He focused on every word I uttered. "Place your hands on the edge and just kick."

Steve followed my instructions to a tee. He was kicking away and splashing water everywhere. We kicked for twenty minutes straight, then I told him to take a break.

A couple of minutes later, I said, "Let's see how long you can hold your breath underwater."

I timed him with his waterproof stopwatch. I was surprised he was able to hold his breath longer than I was. We started splashing one another, and we were really having a lot of fun. I looked at his watch and saw it was getting late. We got out of the pool and dried off.

Steve went upstairs and showered in his room, and I showered in one of the guestrooms. When we got dressed, we left his house and headed to the bus stop. I was tired, and Steve had already fallen asleep during the bus ride. I looked at my watch and saw that it was 5:20 p.m. It had been a long day, and I knew that dinner would be served around six o'clock.

When we got home, I saw my parents reading the

encyclopedia to Tonya and Tyrone. We greeted everyone and went upstairs. No one was really paying attention to us, so I put the action figure and the teddy bear in my room.

Steve asked, "Should we give the toys to them now?"

"Later, after dinner."

We came back downstairs and turned on the television. A sitcom was on, and Steve was really getting into it. He had his eyes glued to the set, and he laughed so hard tears started rolling down his face.

I didn't watch much TV because I thought it was boring. There were so many more fun things to do. Anytime I watched TV, my parents monitored it. We were only allowed to watch learning channels without any kind of intervention. They even had all the pay channels blocked out just in case they weren't around to see what we were doing.

But my radio was all mine. I listened to music all hours of the night. I would always have my headphones on.

Steve turned the TV to this hip-hop program, and we watched the latest videos. Steve mostly concentrated on the words. I directed my attention to the rapper's clothes. I was convinced. When I looked at the cars, the girls, and that house in the video, I saw that if you're jiggy everything in life was fine.

During a commercial, I went into the kitchen and got something to drink. My parents were still reading the children's encyclopedia to Tyrone and Tonya. I knew this routine. After they finished reading, Mom and Dad usually quizzed them. This was their way of seeing if they had paid attention. I overheard them talking about hermit crabs. My parents usually grilled them longer than that, but I saw they were satisfied with the answers Tonya and Tyrone gave.

When I returned to the living room, Steve said, "Gerald, we still have not thought of a science project."

I realized he was right, and I got up. Steve followed me to the backyard. We were both on the grass when I spotted my Frisbee over in the corner. It had been a long time since I had thrown a Frisbee around. I picked it up and threw it to Steve; and he threw it back. I threw the Frisbee over his head, and it went flying to the far end of my backyard. He went looking for it and screamed, "I don't see it."

I screamed back, "It went over into the bushes."

"I still don't see it. Come help me look for it."

I walked over to him, and we looked through the bushes. As he was searching through the bushes, he saw something interesting. "Hey, Gerald. Check this out."

I bent down next to him. We watched as an ant carried a piece of food to an anthill. "Yo, isn't that cool!" Steve exclaimed.

"Yeah, it is."

A light bulb went off in my head. I turned to Steve and said,

"Hey, I found our science project! We're going to make an ant farm and explain how ants work and what they do."

"I don't know anything about ants."

"Me neither. That's what the encyclopedias and the libraries are for," I said. "We'll go next week."

We went back inside, and my mother told us that dinner would be served. Everyone did their duties, and Steve helped me with the plates and drinks.

What an aroma! I knew that smell could only be my mother's spareribs. My mother came out with spareribs, rice, and vegetables. We were all seated, and the only thing left to do was to say Grace. Steve volunteered.

"Lord, thank you for my parents, the Hendersons, the food, and especially my new friend, Gerald. Amen."

Dinner was delicious. I was so full that I wanted to sit at the table for a little bit longer. My father told us all to come to the living room. He popped in an animated movie about five squirrels that were trying to find their way home. My mother asked if anyone wanted popcorn. We raised our hands like we were in school. Ten minutes later, she came back with a huge bowl filled with popcorn and drinks for everyone. We munched and drank while we watched the movie. Tyrone and Tonya sat in between Steve and my parents, and I sat on the couch. The movie was long, and when it ended, I was tired.

Everyone headed upstairs to their rooms. Steve and I went into my room. We got the teddy bear and the action figure and went to Tyrone and Tonya's room. They were getting in their beds when we walked in. I handed Tonya her teddy bear and she got really excited.

"Thanks, Gerald, I love it. I'll name her Sandra."

Tonya kissed me on the cheek and looked over at Tyrone. His eyes were glued to me. Steve took the box he was holding behind his back and handed it to my brother.

"Wow! That's cool. Thanks, Steve. You're the best."

Tyrone jumped into Steve's arms and hugged him. Steve was surprised by my brother's reaction and tried to brush it off.

"Okay, Tyrone, you're welcome. You're welcome."

Steve and I tucked Tyrone and Tonya in and turned off the lights. Steve went to his room, and I went to my room. When I got in my bed, I went straight to sleep.

A knock on my door awakened me at 12:30 a.m. Half asleep, I walked to the door and opened it. It was Steve. I said, "What's wrong?"

"I don't want to sleep in there by myself."

"Why? Are you afraid of the dark?"

"Very funny, man. Nah. I'm just lonely. Can I crash on the floor?"

"Sure, man, come in."

I couldn't get back to sleep, so I just stared at the ceiling for a while.

"I hope you don't mind," Steve said.

"No problem."

"It's kind of cool to have someone to talk to at night, if you're bored or something. It gets lonely when you're by yourself. I wish my parents were at home more."

I couldn't actually relate so I didn't respond. I asked Steve, "Do you go to church?"

"Sometimes, but I don't like going by myself."

"Well, tomorrow, would you like to go?"

"Sure."

"Since we are about the same size in clothes, you can wear a pair of my dress pants, a shirt, a tie, and I have an extra pair of shoes."

"Thanks, but I brought some dress clothes, just in case."

I should have known that suitcase was a little stuffed. I thought this guy was really funny. He had something for every occasion. At that point, I didn't want to continue talking. I visualized Steve showing me up in church and looking better than me.

I tried going back to sleep. I was very restless and fidgeted throughout the night. I got up and headed downstairs to the refrigerator. As I turned around, Steve was a couple of steps behind me.

"Can I tag along?"

It was one o'clock in the morning, and we went outside in the backyard. It was very chilly, and the wind was blowing like a whistle. I came back inside and went downstairs to the basement and got some blankets. When I returned, Steve was just lying on the grass and staring at the sky. "It's a full moon tonight," Steve said.

"Yeah, you're right."

"This is so beautiful. I spend a lot of time outside by myself just staring at the stars, listening to nature. Some creatures only become visible at night. During the day, we don't even know they exist."

We looked up in the sky and gazed at the stars. It was eerie just sitting in the darkness, but I was completely relaxed.

"Gerald, have you ever thought about being all alone and having no one to talk to?" Steve asked.

"No, man, I have my family and a couple of friends."

"That's cool. I feel like I'm all alone and nobody really cares about me."

I was confused. "Everyone likes you. You're the most popular boy in school. People would love to be in your shoes. You have it all."

In a low voice, Steve said, "I guess so." He paused. "Hey,

Gerald, do you think there are different planets out there? Do you think some other kid about our age is sitting outside looking at the stars?"

"Maybe. It sounds possible."

Steve said in a soft voice, "Sometimes I wish I could change places with someone else."

I wanted to make sure I heard him correctly, but he wouldn't repeat what he had said. We sat out there for a while, and I started getting tired. I suggested that we go back inside or else we would never get up in time for church. We quietly returned back to my room. When I looked at my clock, it was four o'clock in the morning. I set my alarm for seven o'clock and went to sleep.

It was Sunday morning, and I awoke as my alarm clock went off. I nudged Steve to him wake up, but he just turned over. I told him he had better get into the bathroom before there was a stampede. He got up half-dazed and went into the bathroom. I started looking through my closet for my dress clothes. The thing about church was, I had to wear dress pants and a tie. I would have preferred to be a little more comfortable. I searched through my closet and found one of my suits. It wasn't that bad, but it wasn't up-to-date either.

I missed church last week because I wasn't feeling well, so I was looking forward to going. I put on my jacket then took it off. While placing the jacket on my bed, I saw it had a noticeable tear. I was angry because that was the only suit I owned. I came out of my room and knocked on my parents' door.

When I entered, I said, "Mom, I have a tear in my jacket."

"Well, honey, I don't have time to sew it now. Wear another blazer."

I was upset because I knew my clothes wouldn't match. So I took out a brown and green blazer, a pair of blue dress pants, black shoes, a yellow dress shirt, and a blue tie. That wasn't my idea of looking jiggy. I hurried downstairs to the basement and ironed my clothes and put them in my room.

While I was showering, my mother came into the bathroom and said, "Honey, hurry up! We don't want to be late."

"Okay, Mom, I'm almost finished."

When I came out, I knocked on Steve's door.

"Come in," Steve said.

"Hey, if you want to iron your clothes, you can do it in the basement."

"That's okay, I'll just use this machine."

"What machine?"

"My steam machine."

"What's that?"

Steve showed me a strange looking object. He plugged it into the wall outlet and steam came out. "All I have to do is put my clothes on a hanger and go over the clothes with this machine and all the wrinkles come out."

That was the first time I saw a steam machine. "All right, I am going to get dressed. I'll come back and knock on your door when we're ready to go."

I went back to my room and put on my clothes. Afterwards, I knocked on my parents' door, but no one answered. Next, I went to Tonya and Tyrone's room, and they weren't inside either. I screamed downstairs, "Where is everybody?"

"We're downstairs in the living room," my father said. "Gerald, let's go. I hope you're ready."

I went and knocked on Steve's door.

"Come in." Steve said.

"Are you ready?"

"Almost. All I have to do is to put on my shoes."

As I looked at what Steve was wearing, I started feeling sick. He had on a nice black suit with a light-blue dress shirt with a metallic blue tie with a metallic blue handkerchief in his jacket pocket.

He was putting on his shiny black shoes with blue socks to match. His outfit looked five times better than my own. We got into the car, and my father started the engine.

Steve said, "Mr. Henderson, is the car running? I can hardly hear a thing."

"Steve, this car may be old, but it purrs like a cat. I take care of it, and it takes cares of us."

The church was not that far from my home, and we arrived in no time. As we parked and got up to the church, I heard someone calling me. I turned around, and I saw it was Max. He didn't come to church very often, but when he did it was more fun. We made our way toward the middle pews and sat down. Max was a couple of rows in front of me with his parents and his little brother. My parents were talking to other church members sitting behind us. The rest of us sat down quietly in our seats. Fifteen minutes later, Mrs. Thompson started playing the organ, and everyone quieted down.

Pastor Sampson walked up to the podium. He was about my father's age but had gray hair and a gray beard. He was a very nice man, and everyone in the church really liked him. "Good morning everyone. Could you please turn the Hymn book to 17?"

Everyone took out their hymnals. Tyrone and Tonya began singing, even though they had trouble keeping up with the words. My mother had a beautiful voice. As she sang, her voice seemed to reach every corner of the church. I was in the children's choir, so I was no stranger to singing and joined in with everyone else.

After the hymn, Pastor Sampson began his sermon. This was a signal for all the younger children to make their way downstairs for Sunday school.

During Sunday school, we were taught Bible lessons, and we read different verses from the Bible. This was a good idea because a lot of the younger children got restless and threw temper tantrums while Pastor Sampson preached. I was getting older so I knew one day I would have to stay and listen to his sermon. My mother told Steve to go with Tyrone and Tonya and to keep a careful eye on them. I thought, "Why can't I go and watch them? Why do I have to stay and listen?"

I liked church, but I often thought the sermons touched on adult themes. I couldn't quite relate to everything Pastor Sampson preached about. That was grown-up time, and I wanted to be with all the other kids. I asked my father, "Can I go with everyone else?"

"Son, sit down and listen to Pastor Sampson."

I started sulking, but when I looked at my mother's face, I decided to smarten up. I didn't want my mother to get angry.

I quickly remembered a time when I acted up, and she smacked me really hard in the back of the head. I was so embarrassed. After that incident, I was teased for a month.

Pastor Sampson began his sermon, "How do you start your day?" Everyone looked around. "Do you start it by worrying about what you have to do, your tasks, your deadlines, or your chores? You should start each day by praising God and counting your blessings."

Everyone responded, "Amen!"

I wasn't listening to every word as he continued preaching because all I wanted was to be around the other kids. My mother noticed. She tapped me and said, "Gerald, are you paying attention?"

I tried to be as convincing as possible. "Yes, Mom."

"Oh, really! What did he just say?" My mother folded her arms.

"Mmm, mmm, mmm." I was at a loss for words.

My mother said, "Just as I thought. The next time I ask you what Pastor Sampson said and you can't repeat it, you'll be sorry."

That woke me up, and I began listening very carefully. Pastor Sampson was going on from scripture to scripture and started talking about material possessions. "Listen, everyone, do you know you can't extract any values from the material world?"

I was confused. I didn't know what he meant by that comment.

He explained, "The material world can sometimes trick us.

People hide behind their possessions because they think it makes them important. I was watching TV the other day. A lottery winner went bankrupt, and no one would lend him a penny to get a hamburger. You know why?" He scratched his head and continued, "People, I'll tell you why. Because when he had all those material things, he thought he didn't need anything else. He thought people just needed him."

Pastor Sampson stopped for a moment, shook his head, and continued. "But people do need kindness, love, generosity, friendship, and fairness. You know what?"

He looked into the congregation as if he was waiting for a response. "People only wanted to be around him because they had something to gain. But when he had nothing, they didn't come around or call him on the phone. I hope this is a lesson to everyone. Please be good to one another and have good relationships with one another. What you represent as a person is more important than what you own. Keep this in mind. The person you may think has everything, may not have as much as you think."

My mother looked at me, and she finally allowed me to go downstairs with the others. She didn't ask me any questions at that point, but I remembered what Pastor Sampson said.

I went downstairs, and I watched as some children played games. Others listened as the Sunday school teacher read scriptures from the Bible. Steve was in the corner surrounded by four girls. He was definitely a girl magnet. Everywhere he went someone talked to him.

I went over to Steve, and he said, "What's up, Gerald? This is Kim, Monica, Maxine, and Sharon."

They barely acknowledged me and continued talking with Steve. I had been going to church just about every Sunday with those girls, and he found out their names with no problem. They were touching his jacket, and another one pulled on his tie.

"That is a hot suit you have on," one said.

I sat in the corner and thought about how things could be different if I was jiggy. Twenty minutes later, the Sunday school teacher gathered us and took us upstairs. I joined my parents, and we made our way toward the exit. My parents were in front of us, and Steve was still saying his goodbyes to his new fan club. Tyrone and Tonya stood patiently next to me.

Traditionally, before we exited the church, we shook Pastor Sampson's hand. I motioned for Steve to come along. When we got up to Pastor Sampson, I introduced him.

"Pastor, this is my new friend, Steve."

"How do you do, Steve?"

"Fine, thanks."

"I hope to see you in church another Sunday with your

family."

"Maybe one Sunday we'll be here."

We headed toward the car. I was relieved that church was over. I began loosening up my tie. It had felt like someone was choking me. As we rode home, everyone was very quiet.

When we got home, I went directly upstairs and made my way to my room. Steve told me he was going to get changed. I decided I would get changed, too. When I got dressed, I went to Steve's room. I knocked and waited by his door. When I entered, he was putting away his steam machine into his suitcase.

While he was putting away his church clothes, I looked at what he was wearing. He matched the colors gold and black. He wore gold sweat pants, a black T-shirt, black sneakers, black socks, and a black hat with gold lettering.

We left his room and headed downstairs into the kitchen. Steve was hungry so we started making a sandwich. I went into the refrigerator and took out the ham and cheese. He took out the mayonnaise. After we ate the sandwiches, we gulped down our juice. He went into the living room and watched TV. I started washing the dishes we left in the sink. I was interrupted when the telephone rang. I dried off my hands and picked up the phone on the second ring.

"Hello."

"Hello, dear. Is that my favorite grandson?"

"Hi, Grandma."

"Yes, sugar. Your grandfather and I were sitting here looking through the family album. I thought about you, Tyrone, and Tonya. Is your mother around?"

"She is upstairs," I said. "Do you want me to get her?"

"Not yet, sugar. How is your new school and new neighborhood?"

"I'm adjusting, Grandma."

"Okay, sweetie. You just hang in there. When was the last time you came to see me?"

"I haven't seen you in about two months."

"Shame on you! I can remember when you used to come over every day after school. We miss you guys something terrible."

I felt guilty and said, "Grandma, I miss you, too. Hey, how would you like to see me today? I'll bring my friend."

"That sounds wonderful! I'll prepare dinner for you both. Let me speak to your mother."

Grandma and Grandpa were my mother's parents, and I really enjoyed being around them. I was so caught up in my new environment that I had forgotten about them. I went to the living room and asked Steve if he wanted to go to my old neighborhood and hang out with my grandparents. He told me that would be cool, and I went upstairs and got my hat. As I came out of my room, my parents came out of theirs.

My mother said, "Gerald, be careful at Grandma's house. Your Dad will pick you guys up when you're ready to come home. I love you, son."

"I love you guys, too."

I knew we had a long trip ahead of us. I went to the refrigerator and got some snacks. I figured we could eat them on the way. After we left my house, we walked down the block and waited for the bus. Sunday schedule was the worst because the buses ran with less frequency. We must have waited forty minutes before we got on the bus.

After the bus ride, we headed toward the train station. We bought our train tokens and waited for the train. Steve was looking around like he was lost.

"What's up Steve? Why do you look so nervous?"

"I hardly ride the trains."

"Man, don't worry. Everything will be cool. I've done this hundreds of times."

As we waited for the train, I pulled out a can of soda and drank it. The train finally came, and we sat together next to a window. It would have been much faster if we had gotten a ride from my Dad. We rode the train for another forty minutes. It was weird, but the whole scenery seemed to darken as we got closer to my old neighborhood.

We got off the train at Belknap Street and went up the subway stairs. My grandparents didn't live that far away from the subway station. My old neighborhood was definitely different from my new one, and this came into sharp focus as we walked down the street. There was litter on the streets and open beer bottles on the sidewalk, and people's spirits seemed completely broken.

We heard a bunch of kids talking loudly as they hung out on the corner. Some of them were smoking and drinking. I recognized one of the boys because he never let me play on the full courts. When he looked over in my direction, he recognized my face.

"Yo, fellows. Look. It's little Gerald. Yo, Gerald! What's up?"

I said, "What's up fellows?"

He said, "Yo, you still play ball."

"Yeah."

"When you get a better game, come check us."

They all began laughing, but I ignored them and kept on walking. Steve and I continued down the street, and we bumped into a couple of girls who were passing by. They looked Steve up and down and started whispering.

One said, "Excuse me cutie, what's your name?"

"Steve."

"Hi, Steve, you looking jiggy."

"Thanks."

I interrupted Steve and told him we should leave.

He said to the girls, "Bye, ladies."

They smiled and said, "Bye, Steve."

The residents living in my old neighborhood weren't as rich as people in my new neighborhood. But most of them always seemed to be in the latest fashions. This always made me really angry. I never understood why parents who made less money than my own dressed their kids in the latest styles.

Fashion was very important in my old neighborhood, but the difference was people were more vocal with it. People teased me all of the time. I was never close to being in style. But in my new neighborhood, I was ignored even more. If I had a choice, I'd rather be ignored than be teased.

As we continued walking, I saw "Ned the Wino" dancing in the street. Ned began his routine whenever he saw someone walking by. He would go into a dancing frenzy and afterwards ask for money. He finished off with his signature line, "I'm hungry, and I am down on my luck. Could you please spare a penny, nickel, dime, quarter, or even a buck?"

When Ned got any money, he spent it on alcohol, never on food. I took out my popcorn and asked Steve if he minded if I gave Ned his soda. Steve didn't mind so I placed it in his hat, and we went on our way.

"Thank you, young man. Thank you."

Steve was extremely quiet, and before we knew it, we had arrived at my grandparents' building. The place where my grandparents stayed was called the Stonewall Projects. I was no stranger to the projects. My old building was three blocks away. My grandparents lived on the twenty-fifth floor. We walked up to the elevator door but noticed a sign indicating that the elevator was out of service.

It was a tiring walk; by the time we reached my grandparents' floor, we were both out of breath. They lived in apartment 25F, and we caught our breath before I rang the bell.

My grandmother came to the door and gave me a big hug. "It's so good to see you, Gerald," she said as we squeezed me close to her body.

"Hi, Grandma. This is my friend Steve."

"Hi, young man. Why don't the both of you come in?"

My grandparents had a nice three-bedroom apartment. It was very spacious inside and was always spotless. We walked into the living room, and I saw my grandfather. Granddad was watching television, reclined in his Lazy Boy chair that we had bought for him last Christmas.

Granddad said, "Hi, Gerald. Come over here and give your grandfather a hug."

"Oh, Granddad, I'm too big for that."

"Oh, really! You're too big, huh? Get over here."

I went over to him and gave him a big hug then introduced him to Steve.

Granddad said, "So how is my daughter, your father, Tyrone, and Tonya?"

"Everyone's fine."

"Next week, we'll invite everyone over for dinner."

My grandmother came into the living room and said, "You men can talk while I start preparing dinner. It should be ready in a couple of hours."

I didn't mind because I wasn't hungry yet.

Granddad said, "How is your new school?"

"School is fine. I am adjusting to my new environment."

My grandfather smiled and said, "That's good. Are you still trying to play basketball?"

"Very funny, Granddad. I've gotten much better."

"Remember who showed you how to shoot the ball."

"Okay, you did," I admitted.

"Can you make any free throws now?"

I said confidently, "Probably more than you can."

"Okay, we'll see. Honey, where are my sneakers?"

My grandmother screamed back, "In the bedroom."

My grandfather was sixty years old but looked good for his

age. He could easily have passed for forty-five. He was six-foot-four and very slim. Granddad worked out three times a week and was always entering marathons. He shouted to my grandmother, "Honey, we're going to the park. We'll be back soon."

"Okay, be back in two hours. I don't want dinner to get cold."

Granddad, Steve, and I left the apartment and walked down the twenty-five flights. At the end, Steve and I were exhausted, but my grandfather hadn't even broken a sweat.

When we entered the park, we saw a lot of people standing around. There were those who came to the park just to hang out. But most people came to the park for basketball, and they played on the full courts. We headed toward the courts on the other side of the park where no one ever went. There weren't any full courts on that side; instead, only single baskets lined up next to one another.

My grandfather asked, "Gerald, are you ready?"

"I was born ready," I said confidently.

"Okay, Gerald, you go first. We'll have twenty shots apiece. We'll see who can make the most baskets."

My grandfather told Steve to count out how many baskets I made. Steve stood near the basket, getting the rebound as I shot. My grandfather sat down near a tree and watched. I went up to the line, bent my knees, and started shooting, Steve counted, "One, two, three, four, five."

My grandfather interrupted. "You did improve."

I made quite a few more shots, and Steve continued counting, "Fifteen, sixteen, seventeen, and eighteen."

I made my first eighteen in a row; then I lost my concentration and missed my last two shots. Steve came up to me and gave me a high five. I said confidently, "Granddad, beat that!"

Granddad said, "Wow! Gerald, that's good! I have my work cut out for me. Can you grant me a couple of practice shots? I haven't shot baskets in months."

I turned to my grandfather, smiled, and said, "Sure, Granddad. Take all the practice shots you need. You're going to need it."

"Confidence. I like that."

My grandfather took a couple of shots and missed them. Granddad wasn't lying when he said he hadn't shot baskets in a while. "Okay Gerald, I'm ready."

I thought Granddad should have practiced longer; his shots really looked terrible. My grandfather went up to the line, and Steve was near the basket getting the rebounds. Granddad began shooting, and Steve counted, "One, two, three, four, five, six."

My grandfather had made six in a row. A couple of shots

later, Steve continued, "Twelve, thirteen, fourteen, fifteen, sixteen, seventeen, eighteen."

I watched in amazement—that was eighteen in a row. I got worried.

My grandfather must have noticed and said, "You look surprised. Let's make it interesting. I'll close my eyes for the next two."

Granddad bounced the ball, closed his eyes, and shot. The ball didn't even touch the rim. It went straight through. If these rims had nets, they would have made a swishing sound. Steve got the rebound and threw the ball back to my Granddad. Granddad bounced the ball one time, closed his eyes, and shot the ball with his left hand. He had the same result as the last shot.

Steve's mouth was wide open. "Wow! That was incredible!"

I ran over to my grandfather, and we both laughed.

I saw an ice cream truck passing by, and my grandfather gave me some money. We sat on the park bench licking our ice cream cones.

We heard loud music blasting from someone's car. The car's stereo system was loud, and the sound was crystal clear. As the car approached, I recognized it was one of the newer sports cars. Steve and I bopped our heads along to the music because we knew the song. He parked near the fence, and when he got out he was jiggy from head to toe. His clothes were so jiggy even Steve stared. I remembered seeing him before; he was a big drug dealer in the neighborhood. A lot of kids wanted to be just like him in one way or another. Some wanted his car, others wanted his clothes, some his money, others his respect; and some wanted all of it.

Granddad saw us staring and said out loud, "It's a damn shame what this community has come to. Boys, I can remember when this neighborhood was as clean as a whistle. Everyone was hardworking and friendly. Drugs and the love of money have corrupted this neighborhood. When I was young, the most important thing was becoming a productive member of society."

"Yo, he's jiggy," I whispered into Steve's ear.

My grandfather interrupted. "Jiggy, huh? Is that all you young kids think about today?"

I was surprised. I didn't know Granddad was so hip.

"Boys, let me tell you something. If you are what you have acquired, then when you don't have those things, you're nothing. A person's worth should not be determined by what he or she has or doesn't have."

After we finished our ice cream cones, we began our trek back to the building. When we got in the building, we walked back up those twenty-five flights. When we reached the top,

Steve and I were breathing really hard. But my grandfather wasn't winded at all. When Granddad opened the apartment door, a sweet smell took over us.

My grandfather told us to get washed up. Steve and I washed our hands and hurried to the table. The table was already set, and my grandmother came out with the food: chicken, spaghetti, rice, salad, and macaroni and cheese. My grandmother started saying Grace. "Thank you for this day, Lord. Bless everyone sitting at this table and our family and friends, near and far. Please bless this food, dear Lord. Amen."

The food was delicious, and Steve's plate was stacked high. I remembered why my mother was such a good cook. She learned from the best. I went back for seconds, and Steve followed my lead.

After the dinner table was cleared, it was time for dessert. Grandma came out with cherry pie and French vanilla ice cream. My grandmother made all her pies and ice cream from scratch. After all that, I was so full that I felt tired.

Granddad, Steve and I went to the living room after we finished dessert. My grandmother went into the kitchen and began washing the dishes. Steve and I watched TV. My grandfather took out his newspaper and read.

Steve suddenly got up and went to the kitchen. I was so occupied watching TV I didn't realize that he was gone for such a long time. When I went near the kitchen, he was helping my grandmother with the dishes. They were laughing and talking up a storm. They looked like they didn't want to be disturbed.

I went back in the living room and sat with my grandfather. He took out one of his old photo albums. I sat next to him as we looked at each picture. My grandfather looked very young in the pictures. I looked at one photo and thought, *what kinds of clothes were those?*

I was glad I wasn't around at that time. Those outfits looked real whack. I looked at another picture, and I saw an older lady and an older man. "Granddad, who's that?"

"Those are your great grandparents."

My grandfather paused and said, "Gerald, those were hard days. As you know, I was born in Jamaica, West Indies, and my parents didn't have much money. Gerald, see that outfit I had on. It was one of a few. I had one pair of pants, one shirt, and for years I didn't have shoes. Many kids were cruel to me because I wasn't jiggy, but back then the word was 'crisp.' They used to laugh at me all the time. They made it really hard for me, but I didn't let them get to me. They even marked my clothes to prove to everyone that I didn't have much. But I had love from my parents, God rest their souls. I always had food to eat, and I was in a loving environment."

I realized Granddad had had it hard when he was young.

"But even though I didn't have a lot of material things growing up, I still felt special. I still was able to capture your grandmother."

I said, "Oh, really! How did you do that?"

My grandfather continued going through the picture album. He stopped at the last page. I saw him standing next to a pretty girl who was well dressed.

"Granddad, who's the cute girl in the picture?"

"Gerald, that's your grandmother."

I was shocked. "That's Grandma?"

"Yup. Gerald, let me tell you a story. Your grandmother came from the other side of the tracks. Her parents had a lot of money and could afford anything they wanted. Your grandmother and I were classmates and played together after school. Her parents didn't want me to play with her. My parents didn't have the social standing they did. Your grandmother's parents were concerned with what others would think. She would always sneak off to play with me every chance she got. When we got older, we announced to her parents that we were a couple. They weren't pleased at first, but they had to accept me."

"Why?" I asked.

"Why? Because I made their daughter extremely happy. See,

your grandmother could have had anyone she wanted, but she chose me for only one reason."

My grandfather paused then shut the album.

"What was the reason Granddad?" I wanted to know badly.

"Because of the type of person I am, not for what I have or don't have. I was down to earth, and she promised me from long ago that she would always love me for me and only me."

I sat back and tried listening, but Granddad always had these long stories. That was the thing about grownups I didn't like. All that lecturing seemed unnecessary.

"See, Gerald, life isn't always about what you have or don't have. Sometimes it's about what you represent."

"Represent?" I asked, baffled.

"Yeah. How you treat others and how you treat yourself."

Steve came into the living room, and we started watching TV again. My grandmother came into the living room shortly afterwards and told me to call home because it was getting late. I called home, and my father told me that he'd pick us up in half an hour. My grandfather told us we should go downstairs and wait for my father. I hugged and kissed my grandmother, and Steve did the same.

My grandmother said to Steve, "Bye, honey. I hope you can come again. Don't be a stranger."

Steve gave her a long hug and replied, "Okay. I'll definitely visit you again."

My grandmother seemed taken by Steve, and I could tell that he wanted to stay around her longer. Steve, Granddad, and I walked down the flights and waited outside the building for my father to arrive. "Ned the wino" saw us outside, and that was his opportunity to start dancing again. He was dancing up a storm in front of us, and my grandfather gave him a quarter.

My father pulled up, and Steve and I told my grandfather goodbye. After we drove off, we waved to my grandfather, who was still standing outside.

My father asked, "So, boys, how was your visit?"

"It was fun, Dad."

"How about grandmother's cooking?"

Steve blurted out, "It was delicioooous!"

We had a long day, and before we knew it, Steve and I were sleeping like babies. My father had to wake us up when we reached home. Steve went upstairs and packed his clothes. I went to my room and crashed on the bed. Steve came out of his room and knocked on my door.

"Come in," I said.

"Hey, what are you doing?" Steve asked.

"Nothing. Are you ready to go home?"

"Yes and no."

"What do you mean?"

"I actually love being around you and your family. This is the most fun I have had in months. I really appreciated you giving me the opportunity to be a part of your family. I enjoyed some of the things you enjoy on a daily basis."

"You're welcome. You can come to my house anytime you like."

"You know what? I also had a great time at your grandparents' apartment. Your grandparents are such good people. I wish I knew my grandparents."

"What happened to them?"

"Both my mother's and father's parents died before I was even born. All my relatives are so spread apart. I don't get to see anyone. You're lucky."

We went downstairs, and my father was in the kitchen. "Dad, are you ready?"

"Sure, let's go."

I was still a little exhausted, and Steve and I fell asleep on the way to his house. My father nudged us when we arrived. Steve told us good night, and we waited until he got in the door before driving off. When we got home, I went straight to my room. Before I got in my bed, I made sure that I had set my alarm clock.

I was in a great mood as I awoke on a sunny Monday morning. I went through my routine, found some clothes, and went downstairs and ironed them. As usual, my clothes were out of style, and after I looked at what I had on, my spirits fell. But my spirits rose again as I thought about being the winner of the contest. I mumbled to myself, "Not jiggy now, but I can be jiggy soon."

I went into the kitchen and ate some cereal and went back upstairs and got my backpack. I was ahead of schedule, so I left before anyone else in the house got up. I walked up the block with lots of energy. As I reached the bus stop, I saw Suzanne.

My morning was going great, and I went up to greet her. She made the bus ride pleasurable, and we talked the whole way there. I congratulated her on making the basket on Friday, and I told her I also made the basket. She then hugged me and kissed me on the cheek. I was so happy! I felt like I was already a winner. As we walked to school, I couldn't stop smiling.

As we entered school, the hallways were filled with noise. Everyone was still talking about the contest. I felt proud to be one of the few who had made the basket. As I walked into homeroom, I saw Ted. He still had that smile on his face. I sat down and briefly talked with the guys before Mrs. Dixon started taking attendance.

"Before we begin, I would like to congratulate Ted, Bill, Steve, John, and Gerald for making the baskets. I wish you all good luck."

Everyone turned around and looked at us. Ted was still smiling. He had to feel good about himself. Most people in the school usually ignored him. I felt good also. I was one of the elite. After homeroom, I went into the hallway and looked over at the JV basketball players who were standing in front of some lockers. One of them saw me looking at him and approached me.

"Hey, are you planning on trying out for the JV squad?"

I hadn't really given it any thought because I had never been on a team before. I didn't answer immediately. I thought back and remembered John and Bill talked to some of those guys earlier last week. "When are the tryouts?"

"Next month."

"I'll try out."

"All right, cool. We could do with another point guard. By the way, my name is Anthony. I am the captain of the team."

After our conversation, I hurried to math class as the bell rang.

Mr. Jones announced, "Class, I have marked your surprise quiz, and I was extremely disappointed. Out of the twenty-three students, many have received low marks. But I do have a few decent ones."

Mr. Jones handed out the papers one by one, and I saw a lot of disappointed faces as people looked at their grades. I wanted to know what I got, and when he gave me my paper I looked at it immediately. I got a perfect score of 115. I tried to keep my smile in as I looked at my paper again.

The day was moving quickly, and I was all geared up for lunch. Like the last couple of school days, Suzanne waited for me in front of the cafeteria. We got our lunches and sat together. John, Bill, and Steve sat in their usual spots and were engaged in conversation.

After lunch, I went to social studies. The lesson was very boring. I didn't pay much attention; I kept looking at my math score so I wouldn't fall asleep in class. I was relieved when class was over, and I looked forward to going to science class.

In science class, Mr. Phillips started calling the teams to the front of the classroom. Each pair explained to the class what they planned to do for their science project. This was a long process, and Steve and I were the last ones to be called. Steve took the lead and explained to the class about what we had planned to do. I went up to the blackboard and drew a diagram illustrating what our ant farm would look like. Mr. Phillips seemed pleased, and we sat down with a sense of satisfaction.

The bell rang, and it was now time for gym. That gave me another opportunity to be near Suzanne. When I got dressed and went in the gym, I saw everyone sitting down. When I looked, Mrs. Julian had set up a mini obstacle course. There were long pieces of rope hanging from the ceiling, twelve tires on the gym floor, eight cones on the floor, and a chin-up bar a couple of feet away.

Mrs. Julian said, "Attention, class. I want everyone to break off into teams. I will explain the rules. First, everyone has to go up the rope and pull the flag down. Get your feet through the tires, dribble a basketball around the cones, up the chin-up bar four times, and finish off with two laps around the gym."

I enjoyed gym. We were always engaging in some kind of fun activity. Unlike my old school, everyone got involved. No one sat and watched. Mrs. Julian's favorite saying was, "Gym is an activity, which means you have to be active."

Mrs. Julian told us that we could pick our own teams. John, Bill, Steve, Suzanne, and I formed a team. Ted and the Geek Pack formed a team because no one wanted any of them on their team. There were eight different teams, and we waited patiently for our turn.

Finally, it was our turn, and we completed the mini obstacle course quickly. According to Mrs. Julian, we were in first place. There was only one team left to go, and that was Ted and his group.

Mrs. Julian blew the whistle, and Ted was up first. I looked at Ted and noticed he had a fire in his eyes that relayed the message of serious business. He went up the rope with the greatest of ease, through the tires, and around the cones, not to mention the chin-up bar, which he went up and down as if his life depended on it. Afterwards, he ran those two laps as though he was trying to break an Olympic record.

Everyone was shocked, and Ted's effort motivated the rest of his team. One by one, the so-called Geek Pack attacked the course like it was a math problem. When it was over, Mrs. Julian told the class that Ted and his team were the winners. Ted and his crew jumped around and gave each other high fives.

The bell rang, and we headed for the locker rooms. The boys' locker room was noisy. A lot of kids were talking about Ted and how his team had had the best time in the obstacle course.

A couple of boys called Ted a geek, and he overheard. I couldn't believe what my eyes saw and my ears heard.

Ted went up to the boys who were talking about him. He said in a strong voice, "Who are you calling a geek?"

One of the boys was laughing and said, "You, you geek!" He then shoved Ted to the ground.

I thought Ted would surely leave the situation alone before he got beat up. But I was surprised; he got as close as he could to the boy's face and said, "My name is Ted!"

The boy went to grab Ted in a headlock, and Ted did this kind of karate move like he was a black belt. He grabbed the boy's hand and put it behind his back and began twisting it. "What's my name?" Ted said in a strong voice.

"Ted! Ted!" the boy shouted in pain.

"Don't you ever call me a geek again! I don't like it! Okay?"

"Okay! I'm sorry. Please let me go, Ted."

I thought the boy was about to start crying. Ted let go of the boy, who sat on the bench rubbing his arm. Ted went back to his locker and got dressed.

His friends saw what happened and one said, "Wow! Ted, who taught you that?"

Ted smiled and said, "I read it in the library."

"Ted, could you teach us?" one of his friends asked.

"Sure, let's go to the library after school."

I laughed to myself. Ted was not playing around anymore. Ever since he had made that basket, he had transformed into another person. I walked into the hallway, and the news had traveled fast. Everyone was talking about what Ted had done in the locker room.

I made my way to English class. We practiced reading comprehension drills for the whole period. I was definitely happy when English was finished, and I remained seated for homeroom. As soon as Steve sat in his seat, I suggested that we go to the library after school to get our research started.

When homeroom was finished, Steve and I left school and waited for the bus. I had never been to the downtown library before. When we entered the library, I realized how huge it was. We asked the librarian which section had books about ants. The librarian pointed upstairs, and Steve and I searched for the books she recommended. We found four books and sat in the quiet room and started reading.

Ted and his friends were also in the quiet room. They were reading the same book. The title was <u>Self-Defense When You Really Need It</u>. They were studying the book like it was a test.

I started to jot down some notes as I read about ants. Steve was doing the same. We were in the library for two hours, and we decided that we would take the books out. I was a little tired, and we left the library and waited for the bus. When my stop came, I told Steve, "Later," and headed home.

I saw Max working in front of the flower shop and decided to talk with him for a while. "Hey, Max, what's up?"

"Nothing, All-Star. What have you been up to lately?"

"School. Guess what?"

"What?"

"My school has a Junior Varsity basketball team."

"For real. Are you trying out?"

"Yeah, but I'm not sure if I should."

"You're not sure? You'd better try out. You're good enough. When you have some time, let me know, and we will do several different drills together so you'll be ready."

"Thanks, Max. Good looking out. "

"Later, little man."

I must have had perfect timing because as soon as I got in, it was dinnertime. I enjoyed mother's tuna casserole, and we had crumb cake for dessert. After my mother and I washed the dishes, I went in the backyard and checked on my father. He was working very hard on the deck, and I decided to help. I hammered in a couple of nails, and soon thereafter I went inside.

I went into my room and began reading one of the books, <u>An Average Day In the Life of an Ant</u>. I jotted down a diagram of an ant farm. I looked at my clock and saw it was getting late. I set my alarm clock, turned off my nightlight, and went to sleep.

It was Tuesday morning, and I woke up at my usual time. I went through my daily routine and left the house. I wasn't quite sure why, but I had a really good feeling about that day. As I approached the bus stop, I saw Suzanne waiting for me.

We got on the bus together and started our morning ritual of conversation. As we walked to school, we continued talking. When we approached the front steps of the school, I felt a sense of security. I really loved my new neighborhood, and even though I didn't have it all, I felt extremely thankful for that moment. As I walked through the front entrance, I looked around at everyone. Everything felt as if it was going in slow motion.

As I entered homeroom and passed by Ted. He said, "What's up, Gerald?"

"Nothing. What's up with you?"

"Nothing much. Isn't life a great thing?"

"Yeah, it is."

"Life isn't fun unless you're living and experiencing different things."

Ted all of a sudden had new philosophies. This was different, especially coming from someone who used to cringe if you called his name out loud.

I sat down, but I wasn't paying attention to what Steve and the rest of the guys were talking about. Mrs. Dixon came in and started calling attendance. Before she reached my name, roll call was interrupted by a message from the loud speaker.

That didn't usually happen, but the assistant principal began with his announcement. "Good morning, boys and girls of

Petree Junior High School. I have some news that will make some people happy."

It was so quiet you could have heard a pin drop. The assistant principal continued. "I have someone that has a message for the students of Petree Junior High School."

There was a big pause in the transmission, and all I heard was feedback from the microphone. That annoying sound had everyone in the classroom covering their ears. The only thing that could have been worse was if someone had clawed their fingernails across the blackboard.

Suddenly someone came on the microphone and said, "Testing one, two, three. Testing one, two, three. Boys and girls of Petree Junior High School."

I wasn't quite sure who it was, but the voice seemed very familiar. Then all of a sudden the person on the microphone screamed out, "OW! OW! OW! OW! OW! OW! OW! OW!"

It was Wildman Bill from WXYZ 91.0 on the FM dial. Everyone in our class yelled back, "OW! OW! OW! OW! OW! OW! OW! OW!"

It was like an echo. It seemed like the whole school was imitating Wildman Bill's wolf call.

Wildman Bill said, "Howdy boys and girls. I just wanted to tell you that today someone is going to win $5,000. I mean five thousand big ones! The second and final phase of the contest is near, and I want only those who made the basket on Friday in the gymnasium to answer the $5,000 question. But people, this is a Petree Junior High School thing, so everyone should come to the gym and support your schoolmates. Maybe we will have a winner this year. This is Wildman Bill signing off. See everyone at 3 p.m. "OW! OW! OW! OW! OW! OW! OW!"

Everyone returned the wolf call. "OW! OW! OW! OW! OW! OW! OW!"

That was the moment I had been waiting for. I looked at John, Bill, and Steve, and they were also excited. Ted had a determined look in his eyes that meant he was ready, willing, and able. Mrs. Dixon continued taking attendance; after she finished, I left homeroom and went into the hallway. The hallways were so loud that it reminded me of a playoff baseball game. Everyone was studying some kind of sheet. Even though there weren't that many contestants, I knew that most people wanted to be part of the contest. If they helped to win, they hoped to get recognition or some of the money.

The day was passing by right before my eyes. Nervous energy rushed through me like I was being electrocuted. When I looked in my notebook, I noticed that I had nothing written inside. During each class, I couldn't get focused on anything. I felt relieved that none of my teachers called on me. I was happy when lunchtime came around. All that nervous energy had my stomach grumbling. As I started walking to the cafeteria, I bumped into John and Bill.

"Hey, Gerald, are you ready for the contest or what?" Bill asked.

"Man, I'm not sure. There are so many hip-hop songs, artists, and years to remember. I feel like my head is going to explode."

John said, "Calm down, man. I'm telling you, everyone in school knows it's going to be a hip-hop song. Just don't worry and study the sheets."

"All right, man. I will study them."

As I approached the cafeteria door, Suzanne stood there with a glow in her eyes. "Hey, Gerald, did you hear the contest is today? Are you ready or what?"

"I guess so. I am not sure if I can remember all those names, years, and artists. It could be a song before my time,"

"I know, but don't worry. Give it your best shot."

While I was in the line for my food, I saw John and Bill reading their sheets. They looked different from the one that I previously saw them studying from. I became angry because they hadn't told me that they had more information. I knew the contest would be every man for himself, but I thought we were all cool. If John and Bill had another sheet then Steve probably had a copy, too. This made me very upset because I thought

Steve and I were friends, and I would never do such a thing to him.

After I got my lunch, I saw Steve still standing in line. John and Bill were already sitting at their table. I told Suzanne to go ahead. I confronted Steve. "How come you didn't tell me about the new sheet?"

"What new sheet?"

"The one John and Bill have."

"I didn't know anything about that."

I felt really stupid. In an apologetic voice, I said, "My fault. I'm sorry for accusing you."

"No problem."

I went back and sat with Suzanne. When I looked over at their table, I saw Steve talking to John and Bill. Ten minutes later, Steve came over to me with the sheet that they were looking at. "Yo, Gerald, you and Suzanne can take a look at this new information. May the best person win."

Suzanne and I thanked Steve, and we studied that sheet while we ate. She was quizzing me, and I wasn't doing too well. I realized that I wasn't as well prepared as they were. My hopes of winning the contest seemed distant, and my chances of becoming the new Mr. Jiggy Man were not looking good. "Suzanne, stop quizzing me."

"Why?"

"I am not prepared," I said. "Suzanne, I am thinking about not even showing up today."

"That's silly. Look, you made it this far; don't be a quitter. How do you know how something is going to turn out until you try?"

"You're right, Suzanne. I'll be there."

I couldn't believe what I had said. I was so scared. I remembered the conversation my father had with Steve when he didn't want to hammer some nails into the boards. I figured I'd give it my best shot and see what happened.

"So, Gerald, what are you going to do with your money again?" Suzanne asked.

"Oh, I am not sure yet."

I didn't want to tell her what I intended to do with the money. She had practically everything. I went back to the sheets and studied away. I came up for some air and looked over to the far side of the cafeteria and saw Ted and his crew. Ted had all kinds of sheets out, and his friends were quizzing him. I was curious to know what kind of information he had, so I got up and emptied my tray in the garbage can near his table. He was answering questions left and right. He even answered questions about songs I didn't know existed.

I walked over to Steve's table, and he didn't look too happy with John and Bill for withholding information. They were also studying their sheets and quizzing one another.

I went back to my table and sat with Suzanne and realized that the pressure was getting to me. I decided not to look at the paper for the rest of the period.

The bell rang, and I went to my next class. The day was still cruising along. Before I knew it, I was back in homeroom. John, Bill, Steve, and Ted had their heads buried in the sheets. I took out my notes and studied, too. John and Bill began quizzing me. I answered most of the questions correctly. I surprised myself and thought, *if they ask me any of these questions, I'll be in good shape.*

Mrs. Dixon came in and started taking attendance. All of a sudden, roll call was interrupted again with a message from the assistant principal.

"Good afternoon, boys and girls of Petree Junior High School. Someone would like to talk to you."

It was none other than Wildman Bill. "Howdy, boys and girls. You have fifteen minutes until I ask the $5,000 question. This is Wildman Bill signing off. OW! OW! OW! OW! OW! OW! OW!"

Mrs. Dixon continued roll call and said, "Good luck, boys. I'll be rooting for all you guys from this homeroom. I'll see you in the gym."

Right after Mrs. Dixon finished attendance, the bell rang, and everyone got out their seats and headed toward the gym. When I arrived at the gym, there were two lines, one for the contestants and the other for the crowd. I felt proud to be one of the select few who had the opportunity to compete for the money.

When I approached the door, one of Wildman Bill's assistants said to me, "What is your name?"

I answered proudly, "My name is Gerald Henderson."

She checked my name on her list, and I entered the gymnasium. It was a totally different scene than I was used to. There were TV cameras and news people everywhere, and there were twenty-five stalls sectioned off from one another. In the middle of all this was a podium with a microphone. As I walked on the gym floor, I looked around. Every seat in the bleachers was filled with people, and a photographer took my picture. I felt like I was at a concert and had backstage passes. All of the contestants lined up in front of the podium. I stood there patiently with all of the others.

All of a sudden, the lights went down low and these colorful lights came on. Then I heard, "OW! OW! OW! OW! OW! OW! OW! OW!"

Everyone in the bleachers began clapping their hands and stomping their feet. Wildman Bill said, "Good afternoon, students, teachers, faculty, and our twenty-five contestants at

Petree Junior High School. Is anybody ready to see someone win $5,000 today? Make some noise."

Everyone responded, "OW! OW! OW! OW! OW! OW! OW! OW!"

Wildman Bill continued, "Well, let's introduce our twenty-five contestants."

This was a long process as he called name by name. After what seemed like forever, he finally called my name, and I stepped forward, waved, and went back in line. All of the contestants found a seat in one of the stalls and sat down quietly. I sat in the front and got comfortable.

The stalls had us boxed in from all angles. The only open space was the front of each stall. I couldn't see anything behind me or at either side. That made it impossible to cheat. There were two rows. The first row had thirteen stalls, and the second row had twelve stalls. On each desk were a glass of water, a pencil, and a single sheet of paper. I felt as if I was taking a scholastic exam. The pressure was killing me, so I picked up the glass of water and began drinking.

Wildman Bill said, "Okay, contestants, you have ten minutes before I ask the question."

The suspense was brutal, and I jumped out of my seat and ran to the exit. I was so nervous. I had to pee really badly. After I finished peeing, I washed my hands. I stared into the mirror and looked at myself for a minute. I glanced at my watch then quickly ran out of the bathroom.

As I entered the gym, I heard counting from the crowd: "Ten, nine, eight, seven, six, five…"

When they reached three, I was seated.

Wildman Bill took the opportunity and cracked a joke. "Boys and girls, we almost lost one. Excuse me, young man. Are you okay?"

I just nodded my head and took another sip of water, which was almost finished. It seemed like a lifetime as I just sat there waiting for Wildman Bill to ask the question.

The bleachers were filled with people. As I looked, I saw Mrs. Dixon, and she smiled at me when she noticed I was looking at her. Several thoughts clouded my mind, and I was more nervous than before. I calmed myself down by taking another sip of water.

As I put my glass down, Wildman Bill came back on the microphone. "Teachers, students, and faculty of Petree Junior High School. Let the games begin. Okay, contestants, here is the $5,000 question."

He continued, "Is everyone ready in the crowd?"

The crowd screamed, "OW! OW! OW! OW! OW! OW! OW! OW!"

"Okay, contestants, this popular song was a hit in the 1960s and number one on the charts for four months. I'll give you one clue. In the background of this song you can hear a whistling sound."

Wildman Bill continued, "You have fifteen minutes to answer the question. Contestants, I will call out the minutes starting from fifteen going backwards. When I reach the last three minutes, I will count every fifteen seconds."

He started his count off, and, before I knew it, he was down to fourteen minutes. I picked up the pencil and stared at the paper for about a minute.

Wildman Bill screamed out, "Thirteen minutes remaining."

I was getting hot under the collar and began sweating. I had studied all those hip-hop songs back and forth, yet the category wasn't hip-hop. I didn't know what to do.

Another minute passed as I thought about the fact that I had no idea what the song was. I was really stumped. I hadn't even been born at the time of the song.

All of a sudden, a light bulb went off in my head. If the song was in the 1960s, that was in my parents' time. It had to be a song in their timeframe. I tried remembering old songs that I had heard. Another minute passed as I thought about that. Then I remembered that old station my father listened to every day over the years. A couple more minutes passed by. I had eight minutes left, and I had nothing written on my paper.

My father listened to so many different songs, it could have been any of them. I started thinking about a whistling sound in the background. Another two minutes elapsed as I thought. I was down to six minutes, and I still drew blanks.

AH! HA! I remembered that song my father played in the car on the way home from Steve's house. I remembered humming and repeating the words that night. I started humming the words, but I still couldn't remember the title. Another minute passed by.

"Contestants, you have five minutes left."

All of a sudden, the chorus of the song came into my head as I continued humming some lines from the song. *Little hummingbird, little hummingbird, that beautiful bird, melody sweeter than any spoken word.*

I put the title down on my paper: "That Little Hummingbird."

I felt relieved. I remembered the title, but the group's name still drew a blank. I knew it started with an "S." My first thought was the Spooners. I thought for another minute and came up with the group's name—it was the Silver Spoons.

I felt a little more relaxed and told myself, *Two down and one to go.*

My thought process was interrupted as Wildman Bill announced, "Contestants, you have three minutes remaining in the contest."

I was now clueless. I didn't know the year of the song. I had to get all three to be the winner. I knew the only chance was to take a calculated guess.

"You have two minutes and thirty seconds left."

At that point, I got really nervous and picked up my glass. When I put it to my mouth, I noticed there was no more water left. I put the glass down and concentrated really hard. I remembered one day that I was in my father's wallet and looked at his driver's license and saw what year he was born. I wrote down 1955 on my paper.

"You have two minutes remaining in the contest."

I thought back to a story my grandfather told me about how my father always listened to his radio when he was around my age. Granddad never approved of the kind of music he listened to. Granddad commented that it all sounded like noise. I thought, *Around my age could be anywhere from twelve to sixteen because at age seventeen my father moved away from home.*

Wildman Bill interrupted my thought process again. "Contestants, you have one minute left."

I knew I had to get the year correct. So I decided, since my father was around my age, I'd use my age. I figured he must have been thirteen when this song came out. I wrote thirteen on my paper.

"You have thirty seconds left."

I quickly added thirteen to 1955 and wrote down 1968 on my paper.

"Fifteen seconds left!"

I erased all of the calculations I made on the paper so everything looked nice and neat. My final answer was "'That Little Hummingbird' by the Silver Spoons in 1968."

Wildman Bill came back to the microphone. "Okay, contestants, time is up. Please put your pencils down."

His assistants came to each desk and collected the papers. I had no idea if what I had written down was right or wrong, but I was satisfied that I had given it my best shot. We all got up out of our stalls and made our way to the front row of the bleachers and sat down.

Wildman Bill and his assistants were looking through everyone's answers to see if there would be a winner for the contest. I sat near John, Bill, and Steve. Suzanne and Ted were sitting farther down in the bleachers. I looked at John and Bill's faces, and they looked extremely disappointed. John was talking to Bill.

Bill said, "Hey, man, can you believe that question? I had no idea what it was. I didn't even write anything down."

John said, "I'm telling you, this contest is fixed. Nobody ever wins. Wait until tomorrow and I see that guy who told me that the category was hip-hop."

Bill was just going off and wasn't paying much attention to me. The atmosphere in the gym was that of shock, most people remained quiet. Every student in the gymnasium thought it would be a hip-hop question. I got up and went to the bathroom. As I walked to the exit of the gym, I looked at all the contestants. Everyone looked upset. Steve had his head down, and Suzanne was talking to her friends.

She said to one of them, "Guess I'll have to try again next year."

Ted seemed to be extremely calm. Actually, he was beaming with confidence.

Could Ted have known the answer?

I had already thought, if anyone could win the competition it would have to be him. I went into the bathroom stall and closed the door. As I started using the bathroom, some other students came in. The bathroom stall had a little hole, and I peeked through and saw it was Ted's friends. I listened as they talked to one another. When I looked again, I saw them giving one another high fives.

One said, "Fellows, Ted answered the question right!"

Another said, "So, what was the answer?"

"It was, 'That Little Hummingbird' by the Silver Spoons in 1967."

I was completely devastated. Ted was always right, and he researched everything he did. I didn't quite know the year of the song so I wasn't that upset. But then again, one stinking year! I couldn't believe I was one year off. After they left, I came out of the stall, washed my hands, and went back into the gym. I took my seat next to John and Bill, and Wildman Bill came to the microphone.

"Let's all give it up for the twenty-five contestants that competed today."

The crowd screamed, "OW! OW! OW! OW! OW! OW! OW! OW! OW! OW! OW! OW! OW!"

"Now the moment of truth is upon us. As you know, no one has won this contest in three years."

I looked over to Ted, and he was still smiling from ear to ear. I was burning inside. I wanted to win that money so badly. I wanted to be the next Mr. Jiggy.

Wildman Bill said, "I am going to tell you the answer to the question. But first, let me tell you this was very close. We had two contestants out of the twenty-five that had two parts of the answer correct. But, unfortunately, only one answered the third part correctly."

Ted knew he was one of the two, and he looked down the bleachers to see if anyone else looked confident. I knew I was the other contestant, but I was sad because I knew that I guessed wrong the last part of the question.

"The title of the song is 'That Little Hummingbird.'"

I knew I had gotten that part right.

"The group is called The Silver Spoons."

That was two out of the three. I looked over at Ted, and he was smiling even harder than before. Being Mr. Jiggy was what I had wanted more than anything else. I didn't need to hear the rest because something I wanted was becoming a hopeless fantasy.

Before Wildman Bill read the answer to the question, all of the lights in the gymnasium went off. There was a spotlight only on Wildman Bill, who was standing at the podium. The rest of the gymnasium was totally dark.

"Boys and girls, teachers and faculty of Petree Junior High School, that magical year 'That Little Hummingbird' by the Silver Spoons was recorded in…"

He paused and looked around. At that point, I wanted to get the whole thing over with so I could go home and go to bed.

Wildman Bill took up the microphone and said, "The year of the song is 1968!"

All of a sudden, the spotlight flashed on me, and Wildman Bill announced, "The winner for this year's $5,000 contest for the name of the song, year, and artist goes to Gerald Henderson!"

I was shocked and sat there paralyzed like a deer that was caught in headlights.

Wildman Bill said, "Gerald Henderson, will you please come up to the podium?"

The lights came up, and I jumped in the air for joy. I screamed, "I WON! I WON! I WON! I WON!"

Wildman Bill shook my hand and congratulated me. As I stood at the podium, cameras were taking my picture. When I looked over at Ted, he smiled as if to offer his congratulations. I stood at the podium, and everyone in the bleachers was making noise. Wildman Bill asked me, "How do you feel, Gerald Henderson?"

"I feel like a $5,000 winner."

He smiled and said, "Another good answer, kid."

Out of the corner of my eye, I watched as two of Wildman Bill's assistants carried a huge check across the gym to the podium. The check was the size of a blackboard and had my name on it. Wildman Bill noticed the puzzled look I had on my face as his assistants approached the podium. He leaned over and said, "Don't worry, kid. The huge check is for promotional reasons."

He slipped the real check for $5,000 in my pocket. When his assistants came over to me, I held one end of the check, and he held the other half. The photographers were still taking pictures, and I was smiling away. John, Bill, Steve, Suzanne, and Ted were my biggest supporters. They were clapping away, and they started a chant in the gymnasium. "Gerald! Gerald! Gerald! Gerald!"

I felt a sigh of relief when they stopped taking my picture. My eyes felt like I had been exposed to a strobe light for hours. A couple of people who were dressed in suits and dresses approached me with pen and paper in hand. I knew that they were the local newspaper reporters because TV cameras were following them. They surrounded me like a football huddle. For the first time in my life, I felt like I was a superstar. I confidently answered their questions. I must have answered a hundred questions as they grilled me. After that session was over, Wildman Bill told the crowd that the same contest would be held next year and the prize would be $10,000.

Ted approached me and said, "Hey, Gerald, I'm happy you won."

"Thanks, Ted."

"I like you. You never teased me or said anything bad about me. I really wanted to show everyone that I could win and I wasn't a geek. I just knew the year of the song was 1967, but after looking through my notes I saw it was 1968. So what are you going to do with the money?"

I paused for a minute and said, "I hadn't thought about it," even though I intended on opening an account at Mr. Smith's store and shopping until I had no money left.

"By the way, you'd better be ready next year because I will be coming for you," Ted said confidently.

I looked at Ted and smiled. Suzanne approached me next and planted a big kiss on my cheek. I was definitely happy, and that added to my victorious moment. Afterwards, John, Bill and Steve came over, and they gave me high fives.

Steve said, "Well, I am glad one of us got the answer right."

John was still a little upset about the information he received and said, "When I see that kid that told me it was going to be a hip-hop question, I am going to ring his neck."

Bill interrupted. "Calm down, man. It's not the end of the world. You know what happens when you assume things."

We all chuckled together, and I really felt like I belonged.

Steve asked, "Hey, Gerald, are you going to get on the bus with us?"

"Nah. I am going to hang around for a little while."

I didn't want anyone to know what I planned to do with the money. I had a big surprise for everyone in school on Wednesday. I was going to be jiggy from head to toe.

Everyone had almost cleared out of the gym, and I sat in the bleachers momentarily. I went into my pocket and took out the check and just stared at it. It read, "Payable to Gerald

Henderson in the amount of $5,000."

That was what I had been waiting for; I couldn't believe it was real. I looked at what I had on, and I knew I would never have to wear that outfit again. I wasn't even going to put on that outfit to mow the grass. My days of mismatched outfits were going to be over. I got up from the bleachers and made my way to the exit. Before I opened the doors, I looked back because this would be a day I would never forget.

I left school and walked to the bus stop with an extra step of confidence. Everything was clicking, and I didn't wait more than five minutes for the bus. I sat back relaxed during the ride. My destination was Mr. Smith's shop. As the bus drove along, I saw a billboard with a different pair of sneakers. I thought, *these must be brand new because I haven't seen anyone with them on and that billboard wasn't there earlier.*

I wanted to be the first one to have them. If I got them, I would have them before Steve. My stop was approaching so I rang the bell. I exited from the back of the bus and started walking toward Mr. Smith's store. When I had a block left to go, I looked ahead and saw Mr. Smith's shop.

The traffic was heavy, and I was very careful as I walked across the street. I heard someone honking their horn. I turned around to see where the honking was coming from. When I looked again, it was Pastor Sampson.

He pulled up to me, got out of his car, and started talking. "Hi Gerald."

"Hi, Pastor Sampson."

"How are you doing?"

"Fine, sir."

"Are you coming to church on Sunday?"

"Of course, I come every Sunday unless I am sick."

"Gerald, I'm curious. When we have different events that help the community, why don't you come?"

"All of the events are on the weekends, and that is usually family time."

"I see, I see. So if I had something going on during the week, would you attend?"

"Sure, Pastor Sampson, I would be glad to."

"I am happy you feel that way; get in the car. I have something today."

I was so close to Mr. Smith's store, and all I wanted to do was to go shopping. I had to put off looking jiggy for another day. When I got into the car and we passed Mr. Smith's store, I was extremely disappointed.

Pastor Sampson struck up another conversation. "By the way, Gerald, I hope I didn't keep you from doing something."

"No, sir, I was just window shopping."

If I didn't go with Pastor Sampson and my parents found out I was looking at clothes instead of doing something more constructive, I would've been punished.

I knew I should have walked faster to Mr. Smith's store. It was definitely bad timing for me, but I knew I could go another time. I was very quiet as we drove downtown. I wasn't quite sure where we were going, so I asked. "Pastor Sampson, where are we going?"

"We're going to a homeless shelter. Have you ever been to one?"

"No, sir."

"Well, we are going to give the less fortunate a good meal and clothes. I do this once a month."

After a short ride, we arrived at the homeless shelter. Pastor Sampson parked around the back, and we opened his trunk. I struggled to take out the bags that were stuffed with clothes. We entered the building and went into the kitchen.

Pastor Sampson handed me an apron. "Gerald, you'll be giving out the rice. Everyone gets a big spoonful."

I went into the cafeteria, and I was in a line with other volunteers. Most of the volunteers were people from my church. I saw people patiently waiting, lined up outside the cafeteria doors. After everyone was ready to serve, the homeless people were let in. I couldn't believe that so many adults with children were homeless. It seemed like some people hadn't eaten in days. I gave a big smile with every scoop I handed out.

Pastor Sampson had an apron on and began going around to each table, praying with them before they ate their food. He was a very good man, and my mother called him, "one of God's assistants."

I started feeling hungry, but knew I couldn't eat. That would have taken food from someone who needed it more than I did.

After Pastor Sampson blessed and prayed with each table, he called me over. "Gerald, come with me to the back so we can set up the clothes in different piles."

He wanted me to separate the children's clothes from the adults'. "Gerald, could you also separate shoes and sneakers in different sizes?"

That was a huge task, and he left me alone to start the process. Twenty minutes later, several other volunteers came and started helping me. Pastor Sampson came in shortly and announced, "We will give these clothes out after everyone is finished eating."

After an hour, I had all the sneakers arranged. None of the sneakers were up-to-date, but they were all in good condition. We were finished, and there was a long line outside the door. We were handing out clothes, shoes, and sneakers. Everyone seemed happy to receive something.

One old man said to a volunteer, "Thank you so much. Now I have a pair of pants that doesn't have a hole in it."

I was standing in front of the sneakers, and a lady came over with her son and daughter. They were so cute, and they looked around Tyrone and Tonya's ages. They were also about their size, so I helped them select pairs of shoes and sneakers. Their mother sat back and watched as I helped them. I asked the little girl, "What's your name?"

She smiled and answered, "My name is Michelle, and that's my brother Paul."

"Hello, Michelle and Paul. My name is Gerald."

I looked down at the shoes they had on, and it was definitely sad. Their shoes were too small for their feet. The shoes had holes on the sides and bottoms, and some of the children's' toes were hanging out in the front.

I noticed how filthy their white socks were. I went to another volunteer and got them a couple pairs of tube socks and some dress socks. I helped them remove their shoes, put the old pairs aside, and put new pairs on their feet. "Michelle, how do those feel?"

"Fine."

"Paul, how do your shoes feel?"

"They are really nice."

They were both prancing around as they looked down at their

feet. Michelle jumped on my lap, and Paul followed. "Thank you, Gerald," Michelle said.

"Bye, Gerald. Thank you," Paul added.

"Bye, Michelle and Paul."

They ran over to their mother and started talking to her. Michelle said, "Mommy, Mommy, look at my new shoes and sneakers."

"Beautiful, honey."

"Aren't they nice?" Paul asked.

Michelle interrupted. "I love them. My feet feel nice and look, Mommy, no holes. At least if it rains, Mommy, my toes won't stick out and get wet."

Their mother came over to me and gave me a big hug and thanked me for helping her children. She had tears in her eyes, and she was holding them back so I wouldn't see her crying.

I felt so materialistic after witnessing her honest appreciation. These kids couldn't care less what kind of shoes or sneakers they were wearing. They were only concerned with comfort and if they had any holes. I continued helping others pick out shoes and sneakers. It felt good helping people.

Two hours later, Pastor Sampson drove me home. I'd had a long day, and all I wanted to do was to go home, eat dinner, and go to sleep. On the way home, Pastor Sampson started a conversation with me.

"Gerald, I want to thank you for coming with me and helping others that are less fortunate than yourself. Did you learn anything?"

"Pastor Sampson, I learned so much about myself and a whole lot of other things today."

"Well, good, I hope you did."

"Thank you for taking me today. A lot of things you said in your sermon last week make perfect sense now."

I didn't say anything else as he drove me home. When we pulled up to my house, I saw something strange. It wasn't that late, but all the lights in my house were off. After saying goodbye to Pastor Sampson, I walked up to my front door, took my keys out, and unlocked the door. It was dark inside, and I wondered where everyone was. I heard a noise coming from the kitchen.

"Mom, Dad. Who's there?"

All of a sudden, all the lights came on and I heard, "Surprise! Congratulations, Gerald!"

I was shocked! When I looked around, I saw my family, Steve, and two other adults who I didn't recognize.

Tyrone jumped on me and said, "Gerald, I saw you on TV."

My mother came up to me and said, "Son, congratulations on winning the $5,000."

My father added, "I guess my music isn't bad after all, huh, son?"

"Dad, your music is the bomb," I said, giving him a big hug.

He laughed and said, "Oh, yes son, the bomb."

Steve gave me a high five and said, "Congratulations, homie, you deserve it. I want to introduce you to my parents. Mom and Dad, this is the person I have been telling you about."

Steve's mother said, "So, we finally get to meet Gerald. Congratulations, young man."

It was dinnertime, and I knew this would be where the celebration really began. Everyone was seated, and my mother came out with the food. I looked at the spread my mother had prepared. She had shrimp, lasagna, fried chicken, baked chicken, steak, vegetables, rice, potato salad, macaroni and cheese, and roast potatoes. I couldn't wait to dig in.

My father began saying the Grace, "Lord—"

Steve's father interrupted. "Excuse me, Mr. Henderson, do you mind if I say the Grace tonight?"

"Sure thing, I don't mind at all."

"First, I want to thank the Hendersons for having our family here. Thanks for showing us that the most important treasure is family, especially our wonderful child, Steve. Bless the food and everyone here tonight."

Everyone looked at each other, and we all said, "Amen."

We were all passing food around to one another, and I was

very happy. I went back for seconds and thirds. Everything at the table tasted delicious. After dinner, my mother came out with cheesecake, pound cake, carrot cake, crumb cake, and ice cream in eight different flavors. My mother's cakes always tasted good, so I ate a little bit of everything. Afterwards, my mother, Tyrone, and Tonya cleared the table.

I looked over at Steve and saw how happy he was to have his parents around. Everyone else went into the living room. I sat next to Steve, and he suggested that we wash the dishes. I told him that would be cool, and we excused ourselves and went to the kitchen. My mother had just started running the water.

"Mom, you can go into the living room with everyone else. Steve and I will wash the dishes."

"Okay, sweetheart."

While we were washing the dishes, Steve said, "You know what, Gerald? Do you know that I was jealous of you?"

I was shocked. "Jealous? For what? You have everything: clothes, a fancy house, a lot of friends, money. What else could you want?"

"Gerald, I would love to have the family life you have. I appear to have everything, but you can't put a price tag on love and family."

Steve paused and added, "You see your parents every day. You share so much with them. You guys are really close. I don't have that at all. My parents are never home, and I don't even have a brother or sister."

He paused again. "Your family makes me feel special. Even when I was at your grandparents' apartment, they treated me like I was related to them. What you have is priceless. I would trade all my clothes, even all the attention, just to see my parents every day.

"See, Gerald, the only reason why my parents give me so much is because they feel guilty about never being there for me. They let me get what I want so I don't complain. But after being around your family, I realized that I need much more."

Everything coming from Steve's mouth was heartfelt, and I carefully listened. He said in a reflective way, "I want to thank you for showing me what's really important in life. You gave me the courage to call my parents and tell them how I really feel and what had been bothering me for a very long time. That is why they are back in town. I told them how important they are to me, and they have promised me they will be in town more."

I thought that was great.

"They said they will still have to go out of town but will schedule trips around family time, instead of work first and me second."

Everything was clicking, and all that thought about being

jiggy now seemed unimportant. I had a lot to be thankful for, and I felt extremely blessed. After we washed the dishes, we joined everyone else in the living room.

After a little while, Steve and his parents headed home. My parents told them not to be strangers, and they said they would come to dinner next weekend. I went upstairs to my room and sat down on my bed after my long and exciting day.

Ten minutes later, someone knocked on my door. "Who is it?"

"It's your father."

"Come in, Dad."

My father came in and sat on my bed. "So, son, you are now $5,000 richer."

I smiled and said, "Yup!"

"So now you can spend your money how you want. You can go shopping and be—what did you call it again?—jiggy."

"That's right, jiggy."

"I give you permission to spend it how you like. It's all yours, son."

"Well, you know, Dad, a funny thing happened to me today."

"What, son?"

"After I won the contest, I was on my way to spend all my money to look jiggy for the rest of the school year."

"So, why didn't you, son?"

"Well, I bumped into Pastor Sampson before I got to the store. He ended up convincing me to help him at a homeless shelter. It was a good learning experience, Dad. These people didn't care if they were jiggy or if their clothes matched. They were concerned whether or not they were warm. They inspected the clothes for tears and the shoes for holes. That alone made them happy. After seeing that, Dad, I felt so shallow. Being jiggy isn't the most important thing in the world. Being a good person is, having people like you for you, not for what you have or what you can do for them. You know, only for you, Dad."

I paused and added, "Pastor Sampson's sermon Sunday about a person who seems as if they have everything but doesn't, was so true."

"How, son?"

"I thought my friend Steve had it all, but he told me how he was jealous of me. He told me he didn't know love and true friendship, and from being around us he experienced both. He told me he now knows what is important.

"Everyone has been telling me being jiggy isn't the most important thing. Max did, you and mother did, Granddad, Pastor, and even Steve. I feel stupid. I didn't understand when you first told me."

"That's okay, son. Sometimes you have to experience things

and figure it out for yourself. There is an old saying that I think is relevant for you. 'I once felt sorry for a man who had no shoes until I met a man who had no feet.'

"See, son, you saw people less fortunate than yourself, and it made you realize what you had and how things can be worse. The most important things are not material. Please remember that you have worth whether you have $6 or $6 million, because we are all human beings and worthwhile in the eyes of the Creator."

I hugged my father and said, "Thanks, Dad. I am going to open an account for my college fund."

"That's a good idea, son. Gerald, you can buy some clothes, but just remember that being jiggy isn't the most important thing in the world."

My father ended the conversation on that note, and I went to bed.

I also like to write poetry, so I will leave you with two poems.

Uncertainty

Yesterday I saw a passerby.
Looking tired he put his hands to the sky.
He claimed that life had been unfair,
Down his cheek rolled a little tear.
Everything I planned has gone astray.
Proclaiming to the Heavens, I've lost my way!
He looked as if he was waiting for a sign,
Rolled up his sleeve and gazed at the time.
Confused and disappointed he continued down the street.
If only me and my destiny could meet.
He sees as a mother weeps of news of a tragedy.
She reminisces over a child, whom she'll never see.
Why have you taken my only son?
He was young, I'm old I should have been the one!
With a puzzled look he began to contemplate.
I have no idea, what is my fate!
Is tomorrow promised, do I have another chance?
Or will I also be the victim of circumstance?
He realized now, nothing in life is a sure bet.
Uncertainty of life is something we must all accept.

Motivation

When I look in the mirror,
What do I see?
A person ready to conquer the world for you and me.
Someone who respects themselves and everyone else.
That is when I truly find myself.
My friends, family, and surroundings are important to me.
Being the best I can is my destiny.